book 2

tim bowler
winner of the carnegie medal

BLADE

CLOSING IN

OXFORD
UNIVERSITY PRESS

OXFORD
UNIVERSITY PRESS

Great Clarendon Street, Oxford OX2 6DP

Oxford University Press is a department of the University of Oxford.
It furthers the University's objective of excellence in research, scholarship,
and education by publishing worldwide in

Oxford   New York

Auckland   Cape Town   Dar es Salaam   Hong Kong   Karachi
Kuala Lumpur   Madrid   Melbourne   Mexico City   Nairobi
New Delhi   Shanghai   Taipei   Toronto

With offices in

Argentina   Austria   Brazil   Chile   Czech Republic   France   Greece
Guatemala   Hungary   Italy   Japan   Poland   Portugal   Singapore
South Korea   Switzerland   Thailand   Turkey   Ukraine   Vietnam

Oxford is a registered trade mark of Oxford University Press
in the UK and in certain other countries

British Library Cataloguing in Publication Data

Data available

ISBN: 978-0-19-275485-1

1 3 5 7 9 10 8 6 4 2

Typeset in Meridien by TnQ Books and Journals Pvt. Ltd.,
Chennai, India

Printed in Great Britain by Cox and Wyman Ltd, Reading, Berkshire

Paper used in the production of this book is a natural,
recyclable product made from wood grown in sustainable forests.
The manufacturing process conforms to the environmental
regulations of the country of origin.

For Rachel
with my love

Blood-sky. Streets dark, houses dark, night dripping down. But the city's awake. She never sleeps. She dozes but she never sleeps—and she sees too much.

Like you.

Don't think I don't know, Bigeyes. You're like some mad insomniac, too nosy for your own good. You pry into what I do, whether I like it or not. Well, I don't like it, not right now. It was different when I wanted company.

Now I got company—plenty—and I don't need

any more. But I guess I'm stuck with you gawping at me.

Who else is watching, though?

That's the question.

There's enough people looking for us. The police, the girl gang, all the others. I don't like to think about it. But the past has come back, hooked its claws into me. Life's dangerous again and I can't just think of myself like I used to.

Becky's walking funny, kind of a shuffle. Can't work out if she's tired or hurt. I know she's scared. She's been choked out since Trixi got killed and Tammy's lot came for us.

She's not a fighting troll like them. She thought she was but she's not. I can't make her out. It's not that I don't care about her. I do—a bit. But I can't crack her. We were getting on good back in the flat but hit the streets again and she chills up.

I don't need that right now. I need her to be strong. But she's turning into a millstone. Sixteen years old and it's like she's got no instinct for anything, not even looking after her kid.

But I guess that's the real reason why I haven't

blasted out of here. If it was just Becky, I'd tell her we got to split. But I can't walk out on Jaz too.

Look at her. Three years old, been living in a drug den and God knows where else, got a dronky troll like Becky for a mother, spends most of her time with dungpots and drifters and duffs off the street, or girls who'd stab you soon as blink, and here she is strolling through the night holding my hand like she's on her way to a party.

Like there's no danger. Like we got a place to go. Only we got no place to go.

Just the future. And what kind of a place is that?

No place for Jaz, I reckon. Not much of a place for me and Bex neither. Not for anyone with a past. And that's the thing, Bigeyes. To go to the future, you got to have a future.

I don't know if I got one. I got my past, same as Bex, whatever hers is, and then I got this—the effing present. Only it's no present you'd ever want. It's dark streets, dark houses, dark city, dark sky.

Becky's looking at me.

'Blade?'

I wish she wouldn't keep calling me that. But it's

too late now. She's worked me out on that one.

'Blade?'

'What?'

'How much further?'

'Not far.'

'What's that mean?'

'About five miles.'

'That ain't far?'

I don't answer. She's been glumming for the last half hour cos I won't tell her where we're going.

She's right and she's wrong. About it being far, I mean. It's not far for her and me. When you got porkers and other nebs tramping on your shadow, five miles is a jink. We got to stuff it out of here quick as fly.

But she's right about Jaz.

Five miles for that little kid's going to hurt. Trouble is, I don't know what else to do. When we left the flat we were snugging out in, I didn't have a clue where to take us. I just said we got to go.

Somewhere away.

That's all I knew. Somewhere out of the city where the porkers and the gang and all those other nebs won't find us. Then I thought of something that might help us on our way—if we can just get there.

Not a great idea but it was the best one I could scrape. So right now that's all I'm thinking of. That and how to get Jaz there—and her dimpy mum.

'Keep going, Bex.'

She glares at me. I take no notice, look at the kid instead.

'Jaz?'

She turns her head, fixes those eyes on me.

'Jaz? Do you want to ride on my shoulders?'

I'm half-hoping she'll say no. She's light as breath but it won't take long for me to get tired if I go too far with her perched up there. She gives me this munchy smile.

I'm telling you, Bigeyes, she melts me, this kid. Doesn't say much, but there's something about her. She's like a pixie or an elf or something.

'Come on, then.'

I hoist her up and she hooks her legs round my neck. I grab hold of her feet.

'You're getting heavier.'

'No, I ain't.'

She's got her arms round the top of my head. She pats me a couple of times on the scalp, funny little pats, like a baby petting a dog.

'Stop that.'

I'm only joking but she stops. We walk on. I can feel Becky watching me. Hard to tell what she's thinking. Mixture of stuff probably. Glad to see me bonding with her kid, or maybe the opposite. But I can't be worrying about that now.

We got to walk. We got to get there. That's all that matters.

'Left here, Bex.'

It's a narrow lane, no lights, no houses. She stops. I can see she doesn't want to go. She's just staring down it.

'What we got to go down there for?'

'Cos it takes us where we're going.'

'And why won't you tell us where that is?'

'Cos it might not work out.'

'You mean it's dangerous?'

Dangerous.

What kind of a stupid question's that, Bigeyes? I want to throttle this troll sometimes. It's like she thinks there's somewhere that's not dangerous for us. Like we can choose this road and not that one and everything'll be all right.

Only it won't. Cos every road, every path, every patch of ground's got danger for us now. We're wanted by too many people, and she knows that as well as I do. But I can't say all this with Jaz listening.

'Bex, I'm just saying it might not work out, OK?'

I lower my voice.

'Look, any way we go's risky right now. We're on the news. People'll know about us. Girl of sixteen, boy about fourteen, three-year-old kid. There'll be descriptions of us. So we got to keep away from people and from CCTVs. We got to keep to lonely places. And this lane's a lonely place.'

Some of the time. But I'm not telling her that.

'Where's it go?' she says.

'Through some playing fields. Then it splits up and one bit goes towards the city centre. We'll take the other bit.'

'Where's that go?'

'To the place I'm aiming for.'

'The place you won't tell me about. The mystery destination.'

Sarky voice but I'm not jiffed about that. I'm more bothered about shifting this troll. She's still blobbed there staring, like she's nailed to the ground.

Then suddenly she looks round at me.

'OK,' she says.

And she sets off down the lane.

I follow, Jaz still perched on my shoulders. I know what you're thinking, Bigeyes. You're wondering why I won't tell Bex where we're going.

Well, you can go on wondering. I know what I'm doing. She's a loose bullet. I don't trust her to do things and I don't trust her to know things.

I don't trust you much either but that's another story.

Down the lane, on, on, darker down here than the streets we just left. This isn't a good place. Better than the streets, less exposed, but not a good place. I'll be happier when the playing fields open up. But that's not for a while yet.

High walls either side, see? There's a school behind that one. Wouldn't know it, would you? Waste ground behind the other one. You'll see it in a moment. I keep clear of this place normally.

Waste ground's got some funny nebs hanging round it—scavengers and druggies mostly, maybe the odd duff looking for something warm to sleep under. Dronky place but what choice have we got? Better among people who want to keep clear of the porkers like we do. They're less likely to give us away.

But we still got to watch ourselves. These nebs might hate the porkers but that doesn't mean they'll like us any better. Becky speaks, low voice.

'There's some people.'

'I've seen 'em.'

'Just ahead.'

'I've seen 'em.'

'Shall we turn back?'

'Keep walking.'

Three figures, slumped against the wall. But they're muffins, no trouble at all. Don't ask me how I know.

'Blade?'

She's whispering now, and she's slowed down, more shuffly than ever. I whisper back.

'Keep moving. It's OK.'

'But—'

'Keep moving. And shut up.'

She does both, somehow. I can see she doesn't want to. She wants to scream her fear into the night sky, and turn and run. She's feeling in her pocket. I can see her hand fumbling about. She's searching for Trixi's flick-knife.

'Bex.'

I'm speaking dead soft. She looks round at me.

'Don't,' I say.

She reads my face in spite of the darkness, pulls her hand out of her pocket.

No knife.

The figures are closer now—two men, dozy-looking gobbos, and a woman swigging from a bottle. They look up, take us in. I give Jaz's feet a little squeeze.

'Say hello to them, Jaz.'

'Hello!' she calls out.

'All right, poppet?' says the woman.

We walk on. I give Jaz's feet another squeeze.

'Good girl.'

She gives my head another one of those funny little pats. She's still light on my shoulders. I'm starting to think I could carry her for ever.

On down the lane, wall on the right falling away. Waste ground opens up. We got to get past this bit quick. I'm hoping there's no trouble but you only want one claphead to start something.

So far, so good. Lane looks clear and nothing in the shadows to the right, nothing dangerous anyway. Just the big heaps of rubbish people dump here in the middle of the night, or whenever the coast looks clear.

'Something's moving,' says Becky. 'By the old fridge.'

'It's a cat.'

'You seen it?'

'I just said. It's a cat. There's another one further off.'

'Where?'

'Behind the pram.'

I nod towards it. Becky looks.

'Can't see no cat.'

'It's just gone.'

She glances at me.

'You don't miss nothing, do you?'

I don't answer. I'm too busy missing nothing.

Another movement among the rubbish. Something low, a body under a blanket. A cough, twitch, wink of light as an eye opens. It fixes me for a moment, then closes again.

We walk on. Hum of the city over to the left. Night hum, like she's moaning, like she wants to rest but can't. I know this sound. I know all her sounds.

But this place is almost silent. Just a pattering among the rubbish, rats probably. Little squeal somewhere behind us, like the two cats just met. But it's soon quiet again. Then another sound.

Footsteps.

Stop, listen. Becky stops too, looks at me.

'What?' she says.

'Sssh!'

Look around. No sign of anyone following, no more steps. Walk on. Sound starts again. Stop.

It stops.

I'm looking all round now, watching cute. Nothing moving on the waste ground, nothing on the lane.

'I didn't hear nothing,' says Becky.

I feel Jaz playing with my hair like everything's OK. Walk on again, slow, steady. But I'm watching, listening, hard as I can. Can't see anybody, can't hear anybody. No more steps, just our own, and the hum of the city again further off.

'I didn't hear nothing,' says Becky again.

It's starting to rain, little feathery drops. Jaz gives a chuckle. I look up. Can't see her clear, just a bit of her face as she leans forward.

'Raining,' she says, and she tugs my hair.

It's like everything's play to her, and for a brief, dimpy moment, I almost feel it too. But it doesn't last.

The footsteps are back.

Stop again, listen, look round. I can feel Becky watching me. I want to throttle her again. She should be watching the lane, the waste ground, not me. She should be checking for trouble.

'What?' she says.

I've seen him now, good way back down the lane, over by the wall. Should have clapped him before. Either he's clever or I'm losing my touch.

He's stopped, keeping in the shadows. Can't make

out his face but it's a gobbo, thick build. Watching me, that's for sure, even if I can't see his eyes.

'What?' says Becky again.

All she's got to do is look. Follow my gaze and look. But she's still watching me. I can feel it. She's just staring at me like a dimp.

'Over there.' I nod down the lane. 'In the shadows by the wall. A guy.'

She says nothing but I feel her eyes lift off me.

'Can't see nobody,' she says.

Jaz tugs at my hair again. I tickle her ankle, glance at Becky.

'Move on, slow. But keep your wits about you.'

We move on down the lane. I don't look back. I'm not going to keep turning. I'll hear him now, even if he creeps after us. But he's not creeping. He's walking loud as you like. Knows we know and doesn't care.

I need to get some kind of a glimpse in case I know him. Not yet though. Got to act confident, like I don't care either.

Only I do. I don't like this stop-start stalking. Almost better if he just came on. But he's keeping his distance, watching but staying back.

Becky's all tensed up again. How she ever got in Trixi's gang's a blind-go for me. She must have done something, shown some bottle, or the trolls would never have let her in.

She's not showing much bottle now. She's choking out again. I can see it. She's gone right down inside herself and she's not coming out.

'Bex.'

I'm listening even as I speak, listening to the footsteps. They're still there, clear in the night in spite of the rain. And they're closer.

'Bex.'

No answer, not even a glance. Now I look back, just quick, enough to see what I need to see. He's closer but still keeping to the shadows. I hear Becky stop.

I do the same, look at her. She's staring back down the lane.

She's got to see him now. He's stopped too and he's still in the shadows but he's much closer than last time she looked.

'Got him?' I say.

She sniffs, turns, walks on.

'Can't see nobody,' she mutters.

She's lying, Bigeyes. I can always tell. And what's worse is she's zipping me over double-time. Cos you know what? There's something I feel as clear as the rain on my face.

She hasn't just seen that gobbo.

She knows who he is.

I'm saying nothing. I'm dead quiet. I'm watching round me, watching Becky. And I'm thinking: first question—if she knows him and doesn't want to tell me, what's she hiding?

Second question—how did he find us? Either it was luck or someone spotted us in the streets and told him. Doesn't matter who. Dregs know dregs. Word goes round, specially if there's money on the barrel.

Third question—if she knows him and doesn't want to go near him, does that mean he's dangerous? I can't make up my own mind about that. I usually know when I see people but I don't with this guy.

Fourth question—if he's dangerous, why's he hanging back?

Maybe he's just cautious, biding his time. Or maybe he's scared too. If he's heard about us on the news, there might be talk about how I'm useful with a knife, how I can throw 'em and stuff. Maybe they're saying this boy's lethal, keep away.

That could help us a bit. Or it could make things worse. Muffins keep their distance anyway. It's the nutters you got to watch, the hard nebs with something to prove.

Or the ones who don't care.

Becky's walking faster, not looking back, not looking at me. Hard to know if she's scared of the gobbo or not. This is stupid. I might just as well ask her.

'Bex?'

'Don't ask me any questions.'

Fair enough. Can't say I blame her. I've been telling her nothing. But Jaz speaks, in that little moony voice.

'Blade?'

First time she's used that name. Doesn't make me feel good to hear it. Not from her. Don't know why.

'What do you want, Jaz?'

'Want to get down.'

'OK.'

I put her down. Feels strange without her up there. She was starting to get a bit heavy but it was nice carrying her. She takes Becky's hand. Becky looks at her, frowns a bit, like she doesn't want to be slowed down. Jaz takes no notice, just smiles. After a bit Becky smiles back at her.

'All right, Fairybell?'

Jaz nods.

I'm looking round again. Gobbo's still there but he's fallen back a bit. He's harder to see than he was but I'm sure he's speaking into a mobile. We've slowed right down now, or Becky has cos of Jaz. Maybe just as well. There's other things to watch for round here apart from the gobbo.

Waste ground's slipping away. Lane's narrowed and the playing fields are opening up on either side. And I'm starting to wonder, Bigeyes. I was going to take us straight on down the lane, then cut off right where it forks.

Now I'm not so sure.

Something about that gobbo's worrying me. He could be all kinds of trouble, specially if he's phoning people about us. He could be talking to the gang or the porkers. He might even be in touch with one of the ticks from my past. He could be one of their hired slugs.

I didn't think so at first but now I'm starting to wonder. God knows how many people they got working for them. There's the gobbo who killed Trixi, there's his mate, and there's that other guy, the big, hairy grunt. And now this new gobbo with his mobile.

He could be one of theirs too. Maybe I was wrong about Bex knowing him. Maybe she's got no idea who he is.

'He's called Riff,' she says suddenly.

I look round at her. She's plodding along, still holding Jaz's hand, but she's watching me.

'That guy.'

'I thought you said you couldn't see anybody.'

'Well, I was lying. I saw him. And I know him.'

I keep quiet. Best not to push her. She's dead tense. She'll tell me if I let her. Push her and she'll close up like a fist.

Rain's stopping but we're walking on through the night. Gobbo's a good way back now. Hasn't moved any further. I can just make him out in the shadows. Think he's still talking on his mobile.

I look back at Becky. She's staring down at the ground, like she thinks she's said enough. I got to prompt her again. But Jaz speaks first.

'Riff,' she says.

Becky glances down at her, then up at me.

'He's a mate of Tammy's gran's,' she says. 'Well, not a mate. More of a sponger.'

I can guess. I remember Tammy's gran well enough. A right old dunny. Anyone could take her for a sky-dive.

A picture floats into my head of that other old lady—white-haired Mary with her scented candles and crazy dog. Nobody would ever call her a dunny. But I can't start drumming myself over that business again.

It hurts too much to think back. All I see is that bungalow. All I hear is the gunshots and the stabbing of my feet as I ran away and left her. There's no way she's still alive.

I got to break out of this, got to get back to what's cracking us now.

'Who's this Riff?' I say. 'Apart from being a sponger.'

'He's harmless. But he knows some scum.'

'I bet he does.'

But at least he won't know anyone from my past. Not if he's tied up with Tammy's gang. I suppose that's something.

'He hangs round with Trixi's brother,' says Bex.

Trixi's brother? I never knew she had one. That's all I need to hear.

'Who's this brother?'

'He's called Dig.'

'Older or younger?'

'Twenty.'

'Mean as Trixi was?'

'You don't want to cross 'im.'

'Turn left,' I say.

'What?'

'Left. Cross the lane.'

I feel her look at me, but I'm glancing back now. I need that Riff gobbo to see us. Trouble is, I can't see him. Don't tell me he's wigged it, Bigeyes. Hang on— I got him again. Still hanging back but he's there.

'Cross the lane, Bex. Move slow. We need that guy to see us.'

She doesn't argue, just starts across the lane.

'Stop,' I say.

She stops, Jaz still holding her hand. They're both looking at me. I bend down to Jaz, give her a smile.

'Riff,' she says.

I don't see her mouth move in the darkness. All I see is those glowy eyes. It's like they're talking instead.

'Do you like him, Jaz?'

She says nothing, just stands there. I'm starting to feel something other than fear. I'm getting flash-backs again as I look into those bright little pools.

'Did he hurt you, Jaz? Did he do something you didn't like?'

I feel myself look away, down the lane to those quiet shadows, then back. Jaz is still watching me, like she's been waiting to answer. She shakes her head.

'Riff's harmless,' says Becky. Her voice sounds harsh in the night. I'd almost forgotten she's there. I straighten up, glance back down the lane again.

'Let's hope he's seen us crossing the lane.'

'What for?' says Becky.

'Never mind. Come on.'

I lead them right across to the fence. It's an easy climb into the playing field beyond and Jaz is small enough to crawl through the little gap in the wire.

'Go through there, Jaz. It'll be fun.'

She doesn't hesitate, just crawls through. I'm over the top by the time she's in the field, Becky just behind.

'Now what?' she says.

'We want to make it look to that Riff guy like we're running across this field.'

'What for?'

'So he can tell that to his mates on his mobile. But we'll cut back further down to the lane, cross it where he can't see us, and lose 'em over the fields on the other side.'

But already I can see that's not going to work.

There's lights moving towards us from both ends of the lane.

Different kinds of lights. Car headlamps behind us,

some way back. But it's the lights coming from the other direction that bother me more.

They're torches, and there's lots of 'em.

They're also some way down but if we'd hung about another minute, one or other of these nebs would have seen us. Trouble is, we're going to have problems cutting over the lane further down with these torch-carriers trigging up.

'Come on,' I say. 'We got to move fast.'

I pick Jaz up and set off.

'Want to walk,' she says.

'Got to carry you, baby, OK? I'll put you down soon as I can. Promise.'

She doesn't argue. Thank God she's a sweet kid.

We're running now. Becky keeps up easy with me carrying Jaz. I'm trying to think as we run. There's still a chance we can double back further down but we got to make sure we're over this field and well out of sight of the lane before we cut right.

And we got to cut right. We can't go into the city again. To get to where I want to take us, we got to go in the same direction as the lane. If we give these nebs a wide enough berth, we could still manage it as long as we keep 'em off our scent when they come looking this way.

Cos that's what they're going to do. I know it.

We're halfway over the playing field. Rugby posts, changing-rooms, pavilion. We run past, but I'm getting tired now. Look back.

Headlights by the fence along the lane, figures standing there. It's porkers—two cars, four nebs, no dogs.

But the torches have gone.

Switched off anyway. They don't want to see the porkers any more than we do. Question is, where are these other nebs? They haven't cut into this field. We're almost on the far side but I'd have seen 'em easy.

And now I'm getting a new pile of thoughts.

Risky thoughts, Bigeyes. Scary too. But they won't let me go. I'm thinking, I got to know more about those torches. They're after us, that's for sure, but who are they?

Not just the three gobbos who were hunting me before. I know that much. I saw at least five lights on the lane. I got to know who these people are.

I got to know what they look like, how dangerous they are.

Yeah, yeah, I know about Bex and Jaz. I know I got to get 'em away. But I got to know who's after us too. I got to know my enemies.

'What's up?' says Becky.

She's looking at me as we run.

'You got something on your mind,' she says. 'I can see it in your face.'

'Tell you in a minute. Let's get clear first.'

We run on. Still no sign of anyone in the field behind us. I got no idea where the torches are now but hopefully they haven't spotted us either. The porkers are where they were before. I can see the lights from their cars burning up the night.

Jaz is getting heavy but we've reached the far end of the playing field. Stop by the wall, breathing hard.

'Down,' says Jaz.

'I know, baby.' I put her down. 'There you go.'

'What now?' says Becky.

'You and Jaz are going to hide behind this wall. There's a way over further down where the brickwork's collapsed a bit.'

'How do you know?'

'I just do. Climb over—it's dead easy—and keep out of sight. There's some bushes on the other side and a little patch of scrubby ground.'

'And what are you going to do?'

'Go back.'

'What for?'

'To check those people out.'

'But we got to get away. You said we got five miles to go to this place of yours. What's it matter who's after us? We know it's people we don't want to see. That's enough for me. It's like one in the morning or whatever and I just want to get the hell out of here.'

I'm looking at her. She's right. We should wig it out of here, for Jaz's sake if nothing else. But it's no good, Bigeyes.

I got to get a closer look at these nebs. I might not recognize any of 'em. They might just be hired slugs. But I got to know what kind of shit's after us.

'Stay here,' I tell Becky. 'And stay quiet. I won't be long.'

She doesn't answer, just scowls. Jaz looks up,

like she's waiting for something.

'She wants a kiss,' says Becky.

I hear the threat in her voice.

I look down at Jaz. Long time since I kissed anyone. Last person was Becky—not this Becky, the other Becky. The ever-special Becky. The dead Becky. But I don't want to talk about that now.

I lean down, give Jaz a kiss on the cheek. Feels kind of weird.

'Bye,' she says, and she turns to Becky like I'm not there any more.

Like I've never been there.

'Jaz? You all right, kid?'

'She thinks you're never coming back,' says Becky.

'What?'

'She's used to people not coming back. That's why she wanted a kiss from you. She thinks you're leaving us for good.'

'Bex—'

'And maybe you are.' Becky looks at me hard. 'Maybe this is it. You don't want us round your neck. You can move better on your own. We're just a nuisance.'

I glance down at Jaz again. She's clutching Becky's leg, pushing her face into the thigh. She's not crying or anything. She's just . . . I don't know . . .

'She's trying to forget you,' says Becky.

I bend down, stroke Jaz's hair. She doesn't move, doesn't look round. Feels strange doing this. I don't like being close to people normally. But it's OK with her.

'Jaz,' I whisper. 'I'm only going away for a few minutes. I'll be back. I promise I'll be back.'

She doesn't turn round, just goes on pressing her face into Becky's thigh.

'Jaz?'

She moves her head, just enough for me to see her right eye. It's got tears in it.

I'm losing it now, Bigeyes. I can't cope with this. I'm thinking, maybe I should just stick here, get us away, forget those nebs.

But it's no good. No matter how much this kid burns me up, I got to know what's out there.

I give her another kiss on the cheek. She doesn't move, doesn't speak.

'I'll be back, Jaz. Promise I will.'

She says nothing, just looks at me with that wet little eye. I feel something drop into my pocket. I know what it is without looking. I glance back at Becky.

'I don't want the knife.'

'Keep it,' she says. 'You're more likely to need it than me. And you know how to use it.'

I reach into my pocket, squeeze the knife, hold it tight.

'Keep it,' she says.

I let go, pull my hand out. The knife feels heavy in my pocket, heavier than it should. I don't know why.

'I'll see you,' I say.

And I'm gone.

Got to think. Got to get back to being me, being strong, being alone. Got to forget about Bex and Jaz for a few minutes. If I'm worrying about them, I'll get snagged.

Check over my shoulder. Becky's found the broken-down section of the wall and she's helping Jaz over it. Least she's doing what she's supposed to. I just hope she waits there till I get back.

OK, got to wipe 'em out of my mind. Got to play stealth.

Still no one in the field, no one I can see anyway. I'm moving low, moving slow, listening hard, thinking cute. I need to head for where the torches were. I know the nebs are still around. I can feel 'em.

The porkers haven't gone either. Their cars are still there, lights on, and I can see two figures in the lane. Cut left, over the hockey pitch.

Stop, look about, listen.

Move on, creep through the bushes, into the next hockey pitch, stop again. Lane's closer now, over to the right. I can see it clearly and even the playing fields on the other side.

I was right not to bring Bex and Jaz here. There's people in this field. Can't see 'em but I can sense 'em. I'm crouched low. I'm like a cat. I'm moving small but ready to spring. I can't run fast so I need all the head-start I can get if they come for me.

Trouble is, where are they?

Got 'em.

Far side of the field where the fence down the opposite end of the pitch meets the lane. Little group of figures, close together, torches off. They must have climbed over and cut back here the moment they saw the headlights coming.

Don't think the porkers have spotted 'em. Probably didn't even see the torches. Hard to tell how many nebs there are in the darkness.

I'm trying to work out how to get close. Best to climb over the fence on the far side of the pitch, then sneak down behind it.

Let's go.

Rain's starting again, soft like before. Feels good on my face. I'm moving slow still, watching the figures all the time. They're quiet. Can't hear any voices. Like they're waiting. For the police maybe.

Or me.

Don't think they've seen me. I'm so low to the ground and I'm keeping well to the left. Now I can hear voices, a deep murmur.

Then silence again.

Sound of an engine revving up behind me. Headlights flashing over the lane. The porkers are leaving. First car's turning in the lane, now the second.

I've stopped. I'm watching 'em drive back towards

the spot where that Riff guy was standing. And I'm wondering where he is now. Cos things are getting confusing, Bigeyes.

Someone's tipped off the porkers about us. Don't ask me how I know. Someone's seen us trigging through the streets and recognized us from the news reports and blotched on us.

It won't be those duffs we saw. They won't want anything to do with the police. And it won't be Riff. He wants us for the gang. It's probably some curtain twitcher.

But then there's these other gobbos. Someone's shunted us with them too. They didn't get here by chance.

I got to find out all I can.

I'm moving again, low, slow. More voices from the figures, louder, more confident now the porkers have gone. But they're still sitting there, in no hurry to blast off.

Here's the fence. Stop, listen. Gobbos down to my right now, half-hidden by shadow. They're in a dip too, kind of a shallow ditch with just their heads and shoulders showing. One of 'em's moving.

Freeze.

He's twisting round. I'm like stone. I'm holding breath, dead still. They've gone silent. No one's talking.

More heads turning. Eyes shifting towards me. I can't see the glints but I can feel 'em splitting the dark, splitting my space. They can't see me. I keep telling myself they can't see me. I'm good at being invisible. That's how I survive.

Only why haven't the heads turned back again? Why are they still staring towards me? I'm low, I'm in the shadow, I'm still, I'm quiet. Why are they looking?

That's when I hear it.

The pad of footsteps coming up behind me.

Shit, Bigeyes. I'm in the grime. I flick my head round.

There he is, sneaking up—and I know him. It's the gobbo who killed Trixi. Tense up, fix him, get ready to spring, left or right. Can't fight him. It's run and run.

Only not yet. Wait till he lunges.

But he doesn't. It's only when he's almost on me that I realize he hasn't seen me. He's watching the gobbos and they're watching him. That's why they turned to look.

But he's still going to see me any moment, unless I keep dead still and he keeps not looking. One of the gobbos calls out.

'Took your time, Paddy,' and a moment later the guy's passed me and with his mates.

Paddy.

So that's his name. Another little detail to add to the picture. Paddy—smooth talker, smooth looker, age about thirty, scumbo, murderer, hired slug.

Sent to bring me back.

Only I'm not going back. Not to where they come from. I'd rather die first.

I'll tell you something, Bigeyes. There's bad places and there's shit places, and then there's hell. And I've been in all three.

I'm not going back.

I'm looking for the other two, the gobbo who was with him before, and the hairy grunt. Trouble is, I can't see these guys clear in the darkness. If Paddy's after me, then the other two must be as well. I got to get closer, got to see 'em clearer, got to hear what they're saying.

I just hope they don't switch their torches back on too soon.

They're talking again, low voices, too quiet to pick out any words. Creep left, not too fast but not too slow either. I got to hear 'em before they split. They could go any moment. And I got to stay hidden.

Here's the other fence. Over or under? I'm looking for a way under. It's safer.

No good. Gap's too small. Check right. Hard to see much now. There's a bush in the way. But that's going to help me too.

Over the fence, dead slow, slither down the other side. No sound of movement from the gobbos, just the same murmur of voices.

Creep on, other side of the fence. I'm close now. I can see the ditch running along the line of the fence. And there's the first of the gobbos.

Stop, stiffen, watch. Inch to the left, just a fraction. I'm lying on my front now, peering through the gap along the bottom of the fence. And there below me in the ditch are six men.

I can see their faces now in spite of the darkness. Three of 'em I recognize straight up—Paddy, his mate, and the big grunt. The other three are strangers but they're tough-looking gobbos. If they're looking for

me too, then I'm in even bigger grime than I thought
I was.

Paddy speaks.

'So nobody's seen the boy?'

I see a shaking of heads.

'We was stuck here,' says the grunt, 'while you
was off with Riff.'

Riff!

These guys know Riff! Shit, Bigeyes. I wasn't
expecting that. And if they know Riff, then they got to
know the gang as well, and Trixi's brother. They must
have made contact some way. Don't ask me how.

But I'll tell you one thing. They won't have told
Tammy that Paddy killed Trixi. They'll have said it was
me or Bex. Maybe that's why they're working together.
More eyes for the hunt.

But the gobbos are playing a game of their own.

The grunt goes on.

'We couldn't move cos o' the police.' He pauses.
'What you done with the other two?'

The other two? I feel a shudder, a hot mist of fear.
Paddy answers.

'I let Riff take the little kid.'

I give a start. It can't be right. Not Jaz. It's got to be someone else.

'And the girl?' says the grunt.

I don't want to listen, don't dare to listen. But it's too late now. Paddy's speaking again. And his words chip open my heart.

'I killed her.'

I feel this pain like I've been stabbed.

I didn't know that was possible. I thought I was dead to caring. But I've been opened up again. Jaz and Becky have walked into my life and now the kid's taken and Becky's dead. And it's my fault. What have I done?

The men are arguing.

'Jesus, Paddy!'

'That was stupid!'

'What you done that for?'

'I had to,' he says. 'She might have talked.'

'But we was told to keep a clean slate. Just go for the boy.'

'I couldn't help it,' says Paddy. 'All right?'

'Like you couldn't help it in the bungalow. And now you done two.'

There's an angry murmur from the others.

'I've hidden the body,' says Paddy. 'They won't find her for a bit.'

They fall silent, like they need to think.

I'm desperate to get out of here. Got to find out what that gobbo's done. It won't be easy. There's loads of places he could have hidden her. Ditches, bushes, refuse tips. But I got to try.

Only I can't just run. I still got to think and creep and play stealth or they'll see me. I can't bear this, Bigeyes. I'm being ripped apart. I'm lying here inches from the nebs who've come to find me and take me back, and the guy who killed Becky, and I'm trying to think, trying to stay calm. But every bit of me's out of control.

Breathe, make yourself breathe.

I breathe, as slow and quiet as I can, only it's juddery and raspy and loaded with the tears I'm trying to hold back. One of the gobbos turns, looks my way.

I can see his eyes, clear as pain. They're bright and dangerous. Can he see me? I don't know. I close my eyes in case he catches the glint. No sound from the gobbos, not even talking.

What are they doing? What's that guy doing? I haven't heard him move, can't feel him coming near. I want to open my eyes but I don't dare. I'm screwing them up tight in case he sees them. I can feel the tears drowning them, drowning me.

I open my eyes and there's the gobbo still watching. He's got to have seen me. Surely he's got to have seen me? Then he turns, lights a cig, and says, 'Let's go.'

The others don't move. I'm watching 'em through blurred eyes. I'm taking 'em in, trying to forget the pain and do what I know I got to do. I'm looking at the faces, fixing 'em in my mind, remembering.

Cos this is where it all changes. This is where I stop being prey.

The grunt's standing up. He looks down at the guy with the cig.

'Lenny's right,' he says. 'We won't find him sitting around. Let's go.'

Lenny—another name. I fix him in my mind, fix and remember. How quickly hate has come back. I thought I'd left it behind but I was wrong.

They're all standing up. Paddy reaches out, takes Lenny's cig, lights one of his own from the tip, hands the cig back. Then he looks round at the others.

'Come on,' he says, and they climb out of the ditch and head for the lane. A moment later, they're gone— and I'm over the fence and racing across the hockey pitch.

I'm still crying, Bigeyes, crying as I run. I should be looking around me, checking for trouble in case those gobbos have tricked me and knew I was there all the time and have cut back from the lane to catch me—but I can't.

I can't even care about that. I'm racing blind, blubbing and screaming and torn up with anger and hurt and fear. I'm over the hockey pitch, over the next, stumbling through the dark and the rain, and here's the broken-down wall, and I'm over.

And they're not there.

How could they be? Every part of me knew they wouldn't be. But every part was hoping I was wrong, hoping I hadn't heard right, hoping Paddy was zipping his mates over to impress them.

Only he wasn't. He was telling the truth. And I knew it all along.

There's no point looking for Bex. She's dead and she's gone and it's my fault. I kneel down on the spot where they last were.

'Bex.'

I'm talking to a shadow but I can't stop myself.

'Bex, I'm sorry. Please . . . I'm sorry.'

I'm staring about me through the tears, trying to work out what happened. There's a stick nearby, a big, heavy thing. Maybe it was that. It would have done the job. One blow would be enough.

I don't want to think about what Jaz saw.

'I'm sorry, Bex.'

I shouldn't have left her. I shouldn't have left Jaz.

'I'm sorry, I'm sorry.'

I shouldn't have gone. I should have taken 'em away from here, kept 'em safe.

I stand up, look round, try to think. Rain's still falling. Wind's picking up. Sky's darker than ever. I'm standing here in the early hours of the morning and I know this is the moment.

I'm on my own again like I was before. I can do

what I planned to do with Bex and Jaz. I can wig it out of here, make my escape. Or I can do the other thing.

Turn hunter.

I don't have to think. I knew the answer the moment Paddy smirked his news. I pull out the knife, flick it open. The blade moistens with rain like it's shedding tears.

'Listen . . .'

I'm speaking low. I don't know who to. Who am I speaking to, Bigeyes?

I squeeze the knife and understand.

I'm speaking to Becky—the Becky who just got killed, and the old Becky, the Becky who knew me, the Becky who died too. And I know they're listening.

I look down at the knife. I can see both Beckys clear, bright in the blade. I close it up, folding the tears inside the hilt. And I speak to them again.

'This is for you.'

I'm running again, back to the lane, and down it. Not the way we came. The way we were going, the way the gobbos are going. I can't see 'em. They're some way ahead. If they haven't cut off somewhere, I'll see 'em in a few minutes, as long as they aren't running too.

And why should they? What have they got to be scared of here? Certainly not a kid like me.

But that's where they're wrong. This isn't their patch. It's mine. My city. They don't know her like I do. And they don't know me, not like they think they do.

On, on, running hard, rain still falling. That's the only moisture left on my face. My tears are on the inside now, and I want 'em to go on flowing. I don't want 'em to stop. I don't want 'em ever to stop.

I'm moving fast now, even though I'm tired. I need to slow down. I'm worried in case my brain stops when I see 'em. If I let anger take over, I won't win. Not with six of 'em. I got to make myself think, plan, watch.

Stop! I've seen 'em—a large, moving shadow far down the lane. They're keeping together, moving quiet, still no torches on. They must have thought I was close when they had 'em on before.

I still can't believe they made contact with Riff and the trolls. I wonder what story Paddy told to make 'em think Becky or I killed Trixi.

But what does it matter? I know who my enemies are. And here's six of 'em walking ahead of me.

No one's looked back. Move to the side of the lane, keep in the shadow, slink and follow. Play stealth. I'm calming down now, turning cool like I need to, but I'm breathing blood.

I'm so dangerous it scares me.

But this isn't the time to act. Keep back, watch, follow. I'm gripping the knife in my pocket. I'm squeezing it. I want to pull it out, flick it open. Memories are flooding me, pictures from the past I don't want to see. But I can't stop 'em. They're filling me up like liquid pain, they're mixing with the tears and the anger and the hate, and the guilt.

That more than anything.

I'm looking at the backs of those gobbos and I'm folding up inside. Cos it's not just the pictures of the past that are coming back. It's the pictures of Jaz being carried away, it's the pictures of Becky lying somewhere dead. Her body must be cold now, cold and wet and growing hard.

And I put her in that place. I left her to die.

I squeeze the knife again.

Don't look at me like that, Bigeyes. Just don't. Don't look at me at all. You don't understand. It's about revenge now. But I got to do it my way.

They're slowing down. The grunt's at the back and he's getting tired. He's strong but he's not fit. Not surprised with all that beef and gut. The others are looking round at him. He's stopped now, catching his breath.

They all stop. Paddy's lighting another cig. They're muttering something.

Freeze!

One's looking back down the lane. Steal closer to the fence, crouch down low. A light flashes on, one of the torches, flicks about, searching. I keep still, keep low. If they come for me, I'll have to blast out quick.

No good wigging it back up the lane. They'll catch me even with this head-start. Best to scramble over the fence and make for the railway line. Easier to lose 'em round there.

But they don't come for me. Torch goes off, and the gobbos move on.

I slip after 'em, slow, slow, close to the fence. I'm deep in shadow and I'm watching their backs, watching for the first to turn round. But they're pushing on, even the grunt, though he's blowing like a gale.

Now I got to watch it. There's more duffs coming into view. Couple just ahead, close to the fence. The gobbos haven't even glanced at 'em but if either of 'em talks to me, it could be hard. The gobbos could hear.

Stop, wait, let the gobbos get ahead. Move on again. Just as well I waited. First duff pipes up straightaway.

'Got yourself lost, kid?'

I don't answer, walk on. I'm nearly past when his mate jumps up.

I've got the knife out before he can blink. It's open and bright and hissing round his face. He steps back, his eyes on the blade.

I hold it still, watching him. I can feel the other duff slumped close by. His mate's still watching the knife, then he shrugs and says, 'Yeah, well,' and sits down again.

I close the knife, put it back in my pocket, move on.

Now's the danger time. Not before when he was facing me. They're both muffins. They can't hurt me. But now they can cause trouble. They can shout abuse. They can make the gobbos turn round to look.

But neither of the duffs calls out.

The gobbos are some way ahead now. Walk on, still keeping back, but I got to keep 'em in sight, got to see which way they go. Right now it's straight on down the lane but they're getting close to the fork where it branches off towards the city or away round the outskirts.

Where I was taking Bex and Jaz. My escape plan. It wasn't bad either. I could still use it if I wanted. But it's no good thinking about it.

Everything's changed now. The past and the present have joined up again.

More duffs ahead, but they're even less trouble than the last two, all of 'em lying by the side of the lane, sleeping or dozing or drugged out. They probably don't even know I'm here.

Walk past, eyes back on the gobbos, another quarter of a mile, and another, and then a mile, and I'm still watching 'em. Why didn't they drive this way? They didn't have to walk up the lane. But I think I get it.

No headlights, no warning. Somebody saw us and tipped 'em off—Riff probably—and they came to meet us, maybe spread out at first with torches, keeping in touch by mobile.

Best that way. Then if the porkers show up like they did, they can split and hide and regroup later.

And there's another thing—they never intended to take Bex and Jaz. If they'd wanted to capture us all, they'd have brought whatever they're driving up the lane. Too much fuss to carry all three of us, especially if we made any noise.

I'm guessing that's why Paddy rubbed out Bex and let Riff have Jaz. He just wants me. Well, he hasn't got me yet.

But here's the fork and there's a van parked on the verge.

The gobbos have stopped.

Freeze, wait, watch 'em cute. I'm still safe in the shadow. They're talking, low voices. Grunt's still wheezing but he's taken a cig from Paddy and he's lighting up.

Rain's stopped.

Creep closer. There's lots I can do but it's all dangerous. Simplest stuff first. Number-plate. Can't make it out. Got to get nearer.

Creep, creep, low, low. I'm hearing the city again. She's over to the left. She's been talking all this time, like she always does, only I haven't been listening. I haven't been able to listen. I've had to keep my wits trimmed on these dregs.

And I'm still doing that, more than ever.

So why'm I hearing the city again? Tell me, Big-eyes. Why'm I hearing her again? A low murmur, like she's not happy cos she can't sleep, like she knows she never will. Or maybe it's just that she's seen too much, too much of nebs like me and them.

Too much of what's going to happen next.

The grunt gives a cough, brings my mind back.

Number-plate. I can read it now. Run over it a couple of times in my mind—done. I'm quick remembering, like I remember all the stories I've read.

Now I'm taking in the other stuff. The van, the

gobbos, the fork in the lane, the rubbish dumped over the fences, the fields stretching away beyond—and then the van again.

I've got ideas flooding my mind but there's only one I care about. It's so strong I can't let it go. Don't try and talk me out of it, Bigeyes.

It's too late for words now. I've got both Beckys in my mind. I'm seeing 'em clear, I'm seeing Jaz, I'm seeing all the other stuff. I'm breathing blood so bad I want to rip up the sky.

Creep closer, through the gap in the fence, down the other side. Gobbos on my right, far side of the lane, lounging, smoking, murmuring. Two of 'em having a pee. Paddy's talking on a mobile.

A rat scudders past me, disappears in the bushes. I'm close to the rubbish on this side of the lane now. It's not so big a tip as the waste ground we passed earlier but there's plenty of stuff for what I need.

Another rat. Stops, looks at me, disappears like the last one. Move on, watching the shadows of the men beyond the fence, but I'm searching too, searching the piles of junk.

I soon find what I want. Shove it under a bush,

move on quiet, slow, picking up stones. Stop at the fence, peer through.

They're still there but they've stopped talking, apart from Paddy on his mobile. They're restless—I can tell—like they want him to hurry up. They keep turning and looking at him.

I'm watching him too, Bigeyes.

You bet I am.

He's finishing his call. He gives a smug little chuckle like everything's OK with the world, like he's never hurt a fly in his life, puts the mobile in his pocket, turns to the others. They're watching him close now.

But not as close as me.

I choose one of the stones, watch, wait. He nods 'em towards the van and they start to move. I throw the stone into the darkness, well over their heads.

There's a soft thud among the rubbish on the other side of the lane.

The gobbos stop.

Not a word from any of 'em but they're staring over the rubbish where the stone landed. One of 'em speaks at last, low voice. But I catch it.

'Probably a cat.'

He doesn't sound convinced.

I wait, watch. They're still staring towards the rubbish beyond the lane, like they're waiting for another sound. Paddy nods towards the van again.

'Let's go. It won't be him.'

A laugh from the other gobbos, a strained kind of laugh. And I'm thinking, yeah—laugh away, laugh your faces off. It won't be the boy. This is the last place he'll be right now.

Laugh away.

I throw another stone, over to the left.

They stiffen, all at once. Now they're really looking, all directions this time. They're not stupid. Even the grunt's looking all round him.

But they don't see me. I'm in a little dip now, just behind the bottom level of the fence. There's bin bags and old tin cans for company but I don't care about that. I can see 'em clear but I'm out of sight for when the torches come on.

And there we go. Six lights flash out.

I dip my head a bit more, just to be safe. But I'm still watching. I'm watching like only I know how to watch. They're still grouped together and they're nervous. I can see it from the way they're standing.

Six big guys and they're scared of an unknown noise.

I could tell 'em about being scared. I could tell 'em about the unknown.

I take another stone. Got to be careful this time. With the torches on they might catch sight of it flying through the air. I wait, watch—and throw, well beyond 'em, deeper among the rubbish on the other side.

The gobbos turn that way.

'Come on,' says Paddy.

And they're over the other fence, all six of 'em, blundering through the rubbish. The moment they're out of sight, I'm over my fence and by the van, knife open. Two tyres'll do. No, make it three. Shit, make it four. Why not?

Zap! Then a sweet hiss.

Three more, then back over my fence and into the dip again. I'm breathing hard but I quiet myself, close the blade, put the knife back in my pocket, check the lane again.

Here they come, one by one, climbing back over the other fence. The grunt's last. He looks bombed out. The others are already by the van, waiting for him.

And I'm waiting for them.

Cos I haven't finished yet. But first someone's got to see what's happened. The grunt does it for me.

'The tyres,' he says.

They look round at him, then down at the wheels.

'Shit!' says one.

They go all the way round the van, muttering, swearing. But I'm watching Paddy's face. He hasn't said a word, hasn't shown a flicker of anger.

He's looking round him again, checking the lane with his torch.

'Spread out,' he says.

Yeah, good move, Paddy. Get 'em to spread out.

Only not you.

I need you here.

They're moving about the lane, slowly, flashing their beams this way and that. I keep low.

Come on, Paddy. I need you over here.

He's stopped, middle of the lane. Three of the gobbos have climbed back over the fence again to search the rubbish on the other side. The grunt and another guy have wandered off, checking the verges.

Paddy's still standing close to the van.

Come on, Paddy. I need you over here.

He speaks, not loud, like he knows he doesn't need to.

'She didn't put up much of a fight.'

He's staring towards my side of the lane. He can't see me. But he might as well be looking right into my face. Cos his words are going right to my heart. As he knows they are.

'You'll find her in a ditch.' He gives a mocking little laugh. 'If you want to bother looking, that is. I wouldn't waste my time if I were you. Life's short. Don't you agree?'

Yeah, Paddy. I agree.

I can see the other torches stabbing the night. But they're no danger. They're in another world. There's only two people in my world right now.

Me and Paddy.

He's looking in my direction, looking hard, and I'm wondering, Bigeyes—is this fate? Or is it me? Can I pull him here by mind alone?

Like that book I showed you.

The Will to Power.

Yeah, the will to power.

Only now it's different. I'm looking at you, Paddy, and I'm asking you—who's got the power now? Who's got the will?

He's still looking this way.

'Come on,' I'm whispering to him. 'Come on.'

He comes on, slow, unsure of himself, flicking the beam of his torch right and left. It falls over the rubbish piles behind me, falls over me even, but I'm still too low for him to see me.

He's close to the fence now.

I slip down to the right, keeping in the dip. The torch goes on searching, but it's missing me altogether. On the far side of the lane I hear the gobbos throwing rubbish about as they search the ground.

'Come on,' I whisper.

Paddy climbs over the fence. All I see of him now is the glare of the torch and beyond that a ghost of what he was. What does he see of me?

Nothing.

Cos I'm a ghost too. I'm doing what I do best.

It's as easy as lifting wallets.

Only this time I'm lifting a man's life.

What'll he see in those last few seconds? Is it like they say? Everything flashing before you as you die? All the things you've done? Or is it just the snuffing of a light, like switching off his torch.

He doesn't see me move, doesn't see me reach under the bush for the cricket bat, doesn't see me at all till I'm right in front of him. Cos I'm not doing it from behind, Bigeyes. I'm doing this right.

He stiffens, opens his mouth.

No words come out. The blow to his stomach has smashed away his breath. Another to the chin, another to the back of the head. He gives a gasp, totters. I knock the torch out of his hands, kick his legs away.

He falls down as far as his knees but he's still upright. He fumbles with his hands but he's dazed, he's not moving right, he's got no guard up at all. He's looking at me, his face as twisted as his heart, and he's mouthing something. Cos he knows what's coming.

Only I don't care to hear.

I look into his eyes. All I see in them is the blood

I've come to spill. I speak. I don't recognize my voice.

'This isn't for Becky. It's for me.'

He doesn't answer. He just stares. He knows it's all over. I drop the bat, pull out the knife, flick it open.

Kiss the blade.

Dawn. Light without light. November sun creeping over the city. But it's dragging darkness with it, like the day's working in reverse. I'm alone, I'm safe, I'm out of sight.

But I'm eating myself alive.

Or dead.

What's the difference? Maybe there is no difference. Life or death, heads or tails. Spin a coin, make your call.

I had to rub him out, Bigeyes. It was revenge. It was right. I had to kill him. Are you listening? I had to kill him.

So why didn't I?

Why's he still alive?

Tell me.

I keep looking at the knife, keep flicking it open,

closing it, flicking it open. What happened? I got pictures in my head but they're dronky pictures, like the ones Jaz draws. They don't make sense.

I got a picture of Paddy's face, his eyes watching me, his mouth pleading. No words, nothing like that, just his lips moving, begging, and then another picture—of me turning.

Running.

It can't be right. I don't do that. I've never done that, not when it's the business. I'm Blade. I'm called that for a reason. I don't mess up. I'm Blade. I'm bloody stinking effing Blade.

Only I didn't kill him. I turned and ran.

Help me, Bigeyes. I don't know what I am.

More sun, more darkness. Everything's inside out, everything's not what it should be. Put the knife in my pocket, look about me . . .

An alleyway, Bickton estate. How'd I get here? Can't remember. Hang on, stuff's coming back. I chose this place for a reason. What was it? Must have had a reason.

Outskirts of the city, that's it. Outskirts of the city, outskirts of the outskirts. Sleepy houses, sleepy nebs.

That's got to be reason number one—nobody watching. What's reason number two?

Think. Make yourself think.

What's reason number two? There's got to be one. It can't just be that the place is sleepy.

Phone box.

That's it—phone box. Got to make that call. Should have done it hours ago, only I haven't been thinking. I've just been drummed out of my brain, slumped here catching shadows in my head. Not doing the stuff I should be doing.

THINK!

Forget about Paddy. Forget about the knife. Forget about what you didn't do. Get your head cranked.

'Phone box.'

That's it. Talk aloud.

'Phone box. Make the call.'

I'm on my feet, peering out the alleyway. All snoozy on the estate but we still got to be careful, Bigeyes. There's plenty of nebs round here with radios and television sets, plenty who'll know about the boy the porkers are looking for.

So far, so good. Curtains drawn across the windows.

All quiet, just the hum of the city further off—and right now I'm glad to hear her. Over the road to the phone box. Check there's a tone—good. Think, breathe, think, breathe.

What kind of accent? I'm best at Scottish.

Nine, nine, nine.

A man answers. I ask for the police. He puts me through. A woman comes on.

'Police emergency services, can I help you?'

Shit, she's Scottish.

'Can I help you?' she says again.

I'll try Irish.

'I've got some information.'

Doesn't sound very Irish but it's the best I can do.

'OK,' she says. 'But could I just take your name and phone number?'

'No, you can shut up and listen. I've got some information and you can have it for free. But if you start buzzing questions at me, I'm gone, OK?'

'In your own time,' she says.

Cool customer. Doesn't sound fazed at all. I bet I do. I'm breathing all jerky, trying to stay calm, trying to stay Irish.

'I've got a number-plate for you. Write it down.'

I give her the details. Thank God I haven't forgotten them. I give her a description of the van, where it was parked, what the gobbos look like. I leave Paddy till last. Part of me wants to keep quiet about him. Part of me wants him to get away so I can have another go at him myself. I won't mess up a second time.

I know I won't.

But I tell her about him. Seems pointless not to.

'Have you got all that?' I say.

'Yes.' First time she's spoken since I told her to shut up. 'And you say this man's name's Paddy?'

'Yeah.'

'OK. So we're talking about six men but you only know two of the names—Paddy and Lenny. Is that right?'

'Yeah, and there's another thing about Paddy.' I'm seeing his face again, seeing the wound I should have ripped across his throat, if only I hadn't spooked out. 'There's . . . another thing about him.'

'Yes?'

'His jaw might be broken.'

'How did that happen?'

'He got hit by a cricket bat.'

'Who by?'

I don't answer. I'm trying to think, trying to keep my accent from slipping, trying not to panic. I've told her too much cos my mind's fizzed.

'Who by?' she says.

Again I don't answer. I'm losing it again. I'm still drummed out of my head, picturing what I should have done to Paddy, what I can't believe I didn't do to Paddy.

Breathe, breathe, make yourself breathe. The woman speaks again.

'I've got everything written down but you haven't yet told me why this information's important.'

Another breath. Long, slow. I make myself speak.

'The girl who got killed in the bungalow in Carnside.'

'Yes?'

'You know about her?'

Stupid question. Course she knows. But she answers in the same quiet voice.

'I know about her.'

'I've heard on the news you're looking for a boy called Slicky and a girl called Becky.'

'That's correct. Is there any information you can give me?'

'I've seen Slicky. All the stuff I just told you—I got it from him.'

'Where is he?'

'I haven't the faintest idea and I wouldn't tell you anyway. But listen—I know him a bit and he's not a murderer. He's just a wacky street kid. He told me he broke into the bungalow for a laugh and found the girl in there dead and this guy Paddy standing over her. And there was this other girl there too called Becky. Slicky and Becky got away and she told him later that Paddy killed Trixi. She didn't do it and Slicky didn't do it. Paddy did it. Are you listening to this?'

'Yes,' says the woman.

I got to ring off. They've probably traced the call by now. Got to wig it out of here quick. But there's one more thing to say.

'Slicky told me another thing.'

'And what's that?' she says.

'Paddy's now killed Becky as well. Hit her over the head or something. I couldn't get Slicky to tell me everything. He just said he was on the lane with Becky and her kid, and Paddy and those men caught up with them. The kid ran away and Paddy sorted Becky. Slicky ran off but he says he saw Becky get killed. Doesn't know what happened to her body. Could be just lying there or maybe dumped in one of the ditches. He wouldn't tell me any more. He just beat it. So you got to bring Paddy in and those other guys.'

'All right. Now listen—'

'I got to go.'

'Wait a minute, can you just tell me—'

'I got to go.'

'Where's Slicky now?'

'That's all you're getting.'

'Are you Slicky?'

I hang up. I'm shaking. I know I've messed this up bad. I wasn't thinking good, wasn't talking good. The accent kept slipping. There's no way that woman believed me.

But she'll follow this up. The porkers got tipped off last night about us being in the lane. They were there themselves. So they'll check this out. They might even bring in the gobbos and find Becky's body.

As for little Jaz . . .

That's something else I got to sort out. But to do that, I got to play stealth again. I got to leave Blade behind me, and Slicky too.

I got to become someone else.

Now this house is a bit different. It's not one of my night-time snugs. I don't ever sleep here. Why? Cos there's a family who live here and they don't go away much—at least, not enough to make it a safe place to snug out overnight.

Big crowd of 'em, noisy as hell. Mum, Dad, and five boys. You got to feel for that woman. Nice enough family but sloppy as a custard pie. Leave stuff all over the place and they got no idea how to keep people out—not people like me anyway.

This is one of my daytime snugs. Haven't told you about them before. I got loads of 'em. More than I got night-time snugs. Handy things, specially when I'm tired during the day and need a chill-pot for a few hours.

The great thing about this family is they're out most of the time. Monday to Friday, nine to five, there's nobody here. He's a bignob with the council, she's a dentist, the boys are at school.

Piece of cake getting in. They got a burglar alarm but they only had sensors put in the hall, front room, and main bedroom. I suppose they think that's all they need. They've obviously got their valuables in those rooms.

But I'm not after their valuables. There's other stuff I want more and it's easy as spit to get at. Quick eye-shine through the garage window to make sure they're all out.

No sweat. Both cars gone and all the bikes. Ring the front door just in case.

No answer.

Right, let's see which of the boys has left a window open this time. There's usually a couple at least. Come round the back.

What did I tell you?

One open there, another one there. Just a fraction and they probably think it doesn't show. You wouldn't believe how stupid some nebs are.

Check round. That's the other good thing about this place—no neighbours overlooking the front or the back of the house. But best to make sure nobody's sniffing about.

All clear.

Ladder from the shed, up against the wall. Another check, then up to the window. This room's shared by the twins. Dimpy kids, mad on football. Same age as me but a goofy-looking pair. Check round again, then whip through the window and pull it back like it was.

Easy.

Freeze and listen. Silence, just the ticking of the clock and the sound of traffic running past the end of the close. Nobody's in the house. Just me.

Me and my pain. Yeah, it's still there. I keep seeing Paddy's face. I had him, Bigeyes. He was finished. He was mine. Why isn't he dead?

He didn't get away. I let him go. I messed up.

Tick, tick, tick.

Bloody clock. I want to smash it up.

Tick, tick, tick.

Calm down. Talk to yourself. Talk aloud.

'Move your stump. Do what you got to do.'

And there's more than one thing I got to do, so there's no time to waste.

'Move your stump.'

Over to the door, check the landing. All quiet, apart from that effing clock. Down the landing, slow, easy, past the oldest boy's room, past the next two bedrooms, on to the top of the stairs. Got to be careful here. There's a sensor down in the hall.

It's never picked me up yet and the stairs are so high I could probably walk right past the gap, but I don't take any chances. Down and crawl. Keep below the level of the top step.

No problem.

Back on my feet and here's the bathroom. Careful again. Main bedroom's close. The door's usually shut but they've left it open this time. The sensor inside can't reach me here but I got to watch myself. I'm not thinking cute like I normally do. I'm too stressed up. I mustn't forget myself and walk past that sensor.

Just as well it's the bathroom we need first, or rather what's in the bathroom. Let's hope Mumsy hasn't used it all up.

I needn't have worried. She's got loads of the stuff left. Look at that shelf—totally crammed. She's even stocked up with more since I last came.

AUTUMN DREAMS
Permanent Conditioning Hair Colour in 20 Minutes

Autumn Dreams? Who writes this stuff? It's hair dye, for God's sake. Still, as long as it works. Don't snigger, Bigeyes. I haven't done this before.

Nourishing multi-tonal colour for rich, fade-resistant
shine

I can't believe I'm reading this. Anyway, let's get on with it.

Scissors. There were two pairs in here last time, a small pair in the cabinet and another on the shelf.

No sign.

Look round—nothing.

Shit, I could do without this. I don't want to have to go looking. Hang on . . .

Behind the shower gel—another pair. Dronky scissors, but they'll have to do. Right, coat off, jumper off, shirt off, lean over the basin—OK, now the scissors . . .

Only they're not moving. Cos I'm not moving. I'm not doing anything. I'm just staring. I'm holding the scissors, like I held the knife in front of Paddy's face as he stared back at me, and here's another face doing just the same.

Staring back at me.

My own face in the mirror.

And you know what, Bigeyes? It looks even more scared than Paddy's did. And I'll tell you something else.

It's like looking at a face I've never seen before.

Yeah, I know—I've seen it. Hundreds of times, thousands of times. Every snug I go to's got a mirror. And every time I see a mirror, I check my face.

It's something I feel I got to do. Might sound dimpy but it's something I got to do. It's not cos I think my face is good.

It's cos I'm frightened it might be bad.

It never is. It's not good or bad. It's just clever. It's clever at not showing what I'm thinking or feeling. It's learnt to do that without me trying. I'm fond of my face. It's a drawbridge. It keeps the world back, keeps me back.

Only not today. That's what's scary. Cos you know what's just happened?

The face has disappeared.

It's just me there instead. Me staring at me. And now the me in the glass is becoming more than just me. It's becoming other people as well. I can see Paddy, and Jaz, and the two Beckys, and Mary, and . . .

And all the other people.

I don't want to talk to 'em, Bigeyes. I don't want to see 'em.

'Go away, go away.'

And there's my face again, like it used to be. Eyes, nose, mouth—everything just like it was. All the other stuff's gone. Thank God for that. I look down at the scissors, snip 'em in the air.

They'll do. Autumn Dreams'll do. And so will I.

I'll do.

What do you reckon, Bigeyes? Too much off the back? I'm a bit worried I've made it too short. But you got to admit the colour's good.

Not quite sure where Autumn Dreams come in. It's red-brown as far as I'm concerned, same as Mumsy's hair. Still, who cares what it's called? It's different and that's all I'm bothered about.

OK, next step.

Back to the twins' bedroom. The great thing about this family is they never use half the stuff they got— and they got loads, as you can see. And cos it's all so untidy, they'll never miss the things I'm going to take. Even if they do, they'll probably just think they've lost 'em.

Right, we need an empty plastic bag. There's always gobs of 'em in this house. They buy stuff from the supermarket or wherever and just leave the bags all over the place. I saw one under the bed by the window when I climbed in.

There it is. Perfect. Nice and big too. Hang on— there's something inside it.

Girlie mag.

Typical. We'll have to use another bag. This is definitely one the boys won't have forgotten and they'll know straightaway someone's taken it. They'll probably think Mumsy's been poking about and that'll freak 'em out but best not to leave any clues, even the wrong ones.

Check round the room.

Can't see any other bags I can use. We'll try the

oldest boy's room. He's always buying games and stuff for his computer. He should have something we can use.

Bingo, loads of bags. We'll take that green one. Back to the bathroom, shove the loose hair into the bag, wash the tiny bits down the plughole, dry round the basin, put everything back as it was.

Now the clothes Mary gave me.

Feels kind of weird getting rid of 'em. Don't know why. But I keep thinking of the old girl, keep remembering how I let her down. But I got to trade the clothes, like I had to trade my hair.

They won't all go in the bag. The coat and the jumper go in, and the shirt, just. No room for the rest.

Back to the big lad's room, grab another bag. I'm tempted to cream one of his jackets while I'm here but it's probably too big and anyway, he's more tidy than the others. He'll notice it's gone.

The twins won't miss anything apart from the girlie mag. All that stuff and you know what, Bigeyes? Most of it's exactly like it was the last time I came, and the time before that.

Not cos they use it and put it back where it was,

but cos they don't use it. They don't even think about it.

Don't ask me how I know.

OK, back to the twins' room. Off with the trousers, socks, shoes. Stuff 'em in the second bag. Right, we got to go for something different from Mary's clothes, something dead different.

And it's got to be things the twins haven't touched for yonks and won't miss.

Open the wardrobe. Check that out, Bigeyes. See what I mean? What's the point having all those clothes if you don't wear 'em? And I'm telling you, they don't. When I see those kids round about, they're either in school uniform or tracksuits.

That's it. They don't wear anything else. And I haven't even shown you the stuff they got inside the wall cupboard and the chest of drawers. But I probably won't need to. There's enough here in front of me.

Right, let's get on with it. Shirt, trousers, belt, socks, shoes, jumper.

How easy was that? Try 'em on.

Good fit too. Better than the clothes Mary gave

me. Even the shoes don't pinch like I thought they would. Just need a couple more things.

Jacket with a hood.

Nothing too flash. Got to be boring so it doesn't draw attention. Not much in here. Try the wall cupboard. Yeah, this'll do. Grey anorak. Yucky but it fits neat. I'll have it. Now the last thing.

Glasses.

Both boys wear 'em and I don't so I won't be able to use 'em much without spooking my eyes. But they might come in handy. The boys have got loads of spare pairs in their desk drawers.

Don't ask me why. They must keep their old glasses every time they go to the optician for some new ones. See? Three pairs in this drawer and two in that one.

I'll try 'em all.

This pair'll do. Bit blurry but I can always tip 'em down my nose and peer over the top. I'll take 'em anyway. Shove 'em in the jacket pocket next to the knife.

Shit!

I've gone all cold, Bigeyes. I'm standing here and I'm frozen up like I'm made of ice. Cos you know what?

I'm touching the knife but I don't remember shifting it.

I don't remember taking it out of my old pocket and putting it in this one. Sounds stupid. I know it does. Stupid to worry, I mean. You don't remember everything you do. You just do stuff and don't notice. It's no big deal.

And this should be no big deal.

Only it feels like one. I don't know why.

I pull out the knife, feel it, stare at it. I don't flick it open. I just hold it, look at it. And suddenly it's like I want to yank open the window and throw the effing thing out into the garden, throw it as far away as I can.

Only it won't be far enough. You know why? Cos no matter where I throw it, it'll find me again. It always does. Don't ask me how I know.

I squeeze the knife, put it back in my pocket. And suddenly I'm glad I didn't jack it. Cos I still got a use for it. If I can just get my brain stitched, I can do what I should have done last night.

I can sort Paddy.

Cos I got to. It's right, not just for Becky but for

me. I got to prove myself again. I can't be weak next time. I got to prove myself. If I can just find the guts.

Guts.

Tiny little word for such a big thing. Bit like fear. Another tiny word, another big thing. And you know what, Bigeyes? It's making me wonder.

Making me wonder if I dare do the thing I really want to do, the thing I always want to do when I snug out here, specially when I'm scared. Trouble is, I'm going to need guts for that too.

Cos to do what I want to do, what I really ache to do, I got to go past the main bedroom, past the open door, past the sensor.

Yeah, I know. It's a spitty idea. It's so risky I'd be bung-crazy to try it. I already got what I came for today. It's time to split, not moon about.

But already I'm walking down the landing. I can't stop myself, Bigeyes. I'm past the oldest boy's room, past the next two, past the bathroom, and here's the open door of the main bedroom, and beyond it, at the end of the landing . . .

The study.

Door open too. I can see right in from here. I can

see the books on the shelves. They look like jewels. I haven't read 'em all. But I've looked inside each one. I know 'em in my own way, like I know all the books in all the snugs I go to.

In my own way.

I'm looking at treasure, Bigeyes. It's glistening back at me. I can see *Sherlock Holmes* and *David Copperfield* and *Jane Eyre,* and that book on the Andes with the photograph of the condors, and *Tao Te Ching,* and *The Diary of Samuel Pepys,* and *Swallows and Amazons.*

Swallows and Amazons.

I love that book. It's a stinger. I can see the cover, the title at the top of the spine, the picture underneath, the author's name in capital letters: *Arthur Ransome.*

Must have been well-brained-up, that gobbo. His book's so good I only have to see the cover and I'm on the lake with John and Susan and Nancy and all the other characters. But it's not enough, not right now. I don't just want to see the cover.

I want to read the book. I want to read it so bad it stuns me.

I hate water. I'm scared of it cos it's big and moving and I can't control it. I don't even want to learn to swim. I just want to stay away from it. But when I read *Swallows and Amazons*, it's like I'm sailing and swimming and everything's plum.

And I want to read it now. I want to forget what's happening for a while. I want to dive into the story, and sail and swim and not be scared. It's worth the risk. The sensor won't get me if I'm quick.

I wait, brace myself, check the gap—jump.

The alarm screams out at once.

Stupid tick! Stupid bloody tick! What the hell was I thinking of?

Back to the twins' room, grab the two bags, push open the window. No sign of anybody below but there's bound to be someone coming to check the house. Out the window, close it like it was, down the ladder, look round.

Still nobody. Then a voice.

'Hello?'

Some guy calling from the front of the house.

Sounds old and nervous. I only just heard him with the alarm going. He hasn't appeared yet so I might still get away if I'm quick.

Whip the ladder back to the shed, slip behind it out of sight, check round the side.

Ancient gobbo standing by the gate. Looks creaky on his feet and he's clearly unsure whether to come round the back of the house. Hasn't seen me yet but he will if I move.

Got to wait. Got to stay put.

Only I can't stay put for long. I got to split. If other nebs turn up, I'm in the grime.

He's coming forward, dead slow, watching all about him. Looks scared, like he's not sure he should be doing this. I'm whispering to him.

'Go back, Creaky. Nothing for you round here.'

But he's coming on. I stay put, keep watching.

He's stopped at the edge of the house, peering this way and that. Definitely short-sighted but he's looking round, checking the garden, checking the house.

'Go back, Creaky.'

The alarm's still screeching away. Sounds demented. I feel like a claphead. Can't believe I was so stupid. I should never have taken such a risk. I should have left the books alone and blasted out sweet and good while I had the chance.

And here's more trouble—another man's voice from the front of the house.

'Jim? You there?'

Just what I bloody need. Creaky's turned.

'I'm in the back garden!'

The other gobbo appears. About thirty, chunky build. Looks a bit handy. Joins Creaky and they both look over the back of the house. And now a third voice.

'Jim?'

A woman this time. She's at the gate before they can answer. About the same age as Chunky. She's holding a mobile phone.

'We're here!' calls Creaky.

She comes round and joins them in the back garden.

'Any trouble?' she says.

'Can't see anything,' says Chunky.

'Then move off,' I whisper. 'Move bloody off.'

They don't move off. They spread out, Creaky

towards the far end of the garden, the woman over to the french windows, Chunky towards the shed.

This is getting bad, Bigeyes. I'm still out of sight but if he keeps coming on, I'm stuffed. Then the woman calls out.

'There!'

But she's not pointing at me. She's pointing up at the twins' bedroom. Chunky stops and turns.

'The window,' she says. 'It's slightly open.'

Both gobbos stare up at it.

'Might have been like that before,' says Creaky. 'You know what the boys are like.'

'There are some marks in the grass,' says the woman. She bends over them. 'Like someone's dug the end of a ladder in it.'

Creaky steps over and looks down.

'We don't know for certain it's ladder marks.'

'Easy to check,' says Chunky. 'They keep it in the shed.'

And he turns back towards me.

'I'm going to ring Mr Braden,' says the woman. 'I've got his work number.'

'And then the police,' says Creaky.

'I'll check out the ladder,' says Chunky, and he comes on again.

I tense. If I stay where I am, he'll see me the moment he reaches the door. If I move to the side to avoid him, I'll put myself in sight of the other two.

But now there are more shouts from the front of the house.

Men's voices.

'Everything all right back there?'

'Need any help?'

No sign of anybody at the gate, but Chunky's stopped, inches from the door. He's turned to look back, and so have the others. Now's my chance, while they're facing the other way.

I fling the bags over the fence into the next garden, then scramble up after them. I try to make it a jump, a vault, but the fence is too high and I have to rough it over. They hear me and turn.

All of 'em, including the two new gobbos who've just poked in from the close.

'Over there!' shouts one.

I drop into the other garden, grab the bags and jet it across the lawn. Great big thing with apple trees down the sides and a pond in the middle. The house is a long way down and just as well. I'm hoping nobody there's heard the shouting, even if they've snagged the sound of the alarm.

No sign of anyone at the windows yet but I'm checking 'em good as I belt on.

I'm not looking back at all. I've jerked the hood over my head and I'm wigging it as fast as I can go. Not fast enough though.

'There he is!' comes a shout behind me.

And now there's a face at one of the upstairs windows.

An old dunny peering out at me. Looks frightened. She's holding a phone and dialling a number. A young man appears next to her, then another, then a boy.

They disappear from view as I tear down the side of the house. I hear shouts from inside.

'I'll cut him off at the front!'

One of the guys but I don't stop to think. I reach the front of the house. Nobody there yet but I can hear footsteps pounding on the staircase. There's a mountain bike propped outside the front door. Got to be the boy's.

'Thanks, mate.'

I hook the bags onto the handlebars, shove the bike out of the gate. The front door bursts open and the two guys thunder out.

'Hoy!' bellows one.

But I'm already pedalling like death.

More shouts behind me, some from the gobbos in the doorway, some from Chunky. He's run all the way round to where the close meets the street. Yelling either side of me too, doors and windows opening right and left.

Sound of a car starting behind me.

Got to get off the street.

Another car starting.

I look about me. I know this place. There's an alley just ahead that runs down the side of the children's playground. I put on speed. Revving behind me, the roar of engines. They'll be here in seconds but here's the playground, here's the alley.

Young woman blocking the way, bending over a little girl. Cute kid, Jaz's age. Mum's fixing her coat for her. I hear the engines close behind.

'Get out the way!' I scream.

Mum looks up, stares in horror.

The engines grow louder.

'Get out the way!'

She bundles the kid to the side. I shoot off the road and into the alley. Behind me I hear brakes screech, doors slam, then shouts from the men, screams from the woman, burning like hate inside my head.

I pedal on and don't look back.

Two minutes later I'm through the alley and racing down Westbury Drive. Nobody after me but I can't stick around here. Anyone who knows where the alley leads can work out where I am. I got to get off the road quick.

Not yet though. Nowhere to dive just here. I got to get to Merton Crescent, take the footpath towards the allotments and dump the gear. After that I know what I got to do.

No compromise there.

Nothing's changed, Bigeyes. I might be drummed out of my head and making mistakes but I'm still guffed over Bex and Jaz. I'm still breathing blood over Paddy.

Here's Merton Crescent.

So far, so good. No sign of pursuit, no funny looks from people in the street. Down to the end, through the gap to the footpath, off the bike.

Got to be careful now. Got to fade into the air, leave no pictures behind. The anorak's a problem. I still got the hood up so no one's seen much of my face or hair but Chunky or Creaky are bound to report the jacket.

So I got to sort that.

Bike against the wall, check round. All quiet on the footpath. Nip back to the gap, peer round Merton Crescent. Sleepy little road but I don't trust the windows. Too watchful.

Back to the bike, wheel it further down the footpath, stop again. Check both ways. Nobody in sight. Check over the walls. Back gardens either side, nobody in 'em.

House on the left looks empty. Windows closed, no lights, no noise. Feels pretty safe. Other one's got the back door open. Grab the carrier bags, lean the bike against the wall, check round again.

Looks good.

Over the wall into the first garden, down the side of the house, open the dustbin. Couldn't be better—half-full, mostly binbags. Take off the anorak, pull out the glasses, pull out the knife.

And there's that feeling again.

Shit, Bigeyes, am I going to get this every time I touch a knife? I never used to. I just did what I did and it was a whack. Now I'm shivering and seeing Paddy gibbering at me in the darkness.

I don't want to see that scumbo's face. And if I got to see it, I don't want to see it like it was last night. I want to see it like it's going to be when I've finished with him.

A dead face, a ripped-up face. Cos you better believe it, Bigeyes, that's how it's going to be. If I can just zap it.

Slip the knife into my trouser pocket, pull out some of the binbags, check round again. No sounds from inside the house, no sign of anyone watching. Drop the jacket and carrier bags into the bin, shove 'em right down, dump the binbags on top.

Perfect. Looks just like it did.

Close the lid, put on the glasses, tip 'em down

so I can see over the top. Back to the footpath, wheel the bike towards the allotments.

I know what you're thinking, Bigeyes. You're thinking why keep the bike when they saw that too? Well, you can go on thinking. I don't have to explain everything to you.

All right, stop glumming. I'll tell you.

I need the bike a bit longer, OK? Risky, I know, but I got some distance to go and time's ticking. We'll have to walk past the allotments but once they're behind us, I can ride. And if I keep to the quiet roads, I should be all right.

Allotments opening up already, see? Nice and empty, apart from that old gobbo at the far end and he's just a muffin. Even so, I got to keep a good watch. Walk on, sniping round. No sign of any trouble but I'm feeling edgy.

Bike's making a noise, kind of a tickety-tick. Twig caught in the spokes. Bend down, pull it out, straighten up, see two figures ahead.

Gobbos.

Middle-aged and probably muffins but I'm watching 'em cute. They're coming on. I push the bike forward, not too fast, not too slow. They're looking me over. I know what's coming. One of 'em's going to ask me why I'm not in school.

But I'm wrong.

They're past and gone without a word.

On down the footpath and through to Cutnall Close. Back on the bike and away, out to the main road, over that and off down the lanes towards the eastern suburbs.

It's getting colder and I'm starting to miss that jacket. Sky's darker too. More rain coming. I put on speed. Need to get there before it comes down.

But it's already spitting.

Into the Cliffsea estate, past the shops, down Langdon Drive, onto the track by the football pitch. Down to the end, stop by the bushes, check round.

No sign of anyone. Check again, check good. All clear.

Heave the bike into the bushes.

I kick it well under the foliage and step back. Good and buried. You can't see it at all from the track. You'd have to walk right up to the bushes and even then you might miss it.

Got to move. Rain's getting heavier. Just as well we haven't got far to go. Over the stile and left down the lane towards Marsh View.

Don't ask me why they call it that. There's nothing in the way of marsh round here and not much of a view either. But it's not a bad name for a smelly block of flats on the backside of an estate.

Cos that's what it is. See it? That dronky building is Marsh View.

And I'll tell you something else, Bigeyes.

It's where I was bringing us last night. The place I wouldn't tell Bex about. You were probably wondering why, like she was.

Well, I had a plan. Or kind of a plan.

I could still use it for myself if I wanted to. To get away, I mean. Only we both know I won't. That plan's stuffed now so I'll use it for something else.

OK, walk on. Got to be super-cute now. Got to walk small, walk dark, walk invisible. Best no one sees us come and go. And if they do, best they don't remember us. So watch out. It's a funny little estate. Mostly sleepers but there's nosy nebs here too.

Close now. Keep walking, head down, low and

slow, easy pace. Snipe left and right. Just as well it's raining. Nobody out now apart from those two women on the other pavement, and they're hurrying away.

Can't use these glasses any more. They're doing my head in, specially now they're wet. Chuck 'em in the bin, walk on, nice and slow, nice and casual. Here we are.

Marsh End.

What did I tell you, Bigeyes? Dronky or what? You'd have to be brain-dead to live in a place like this. Lucky for us, there's one guy who is. But we're not here to see his flat.

We're here to nick his car.

Never mind how I'm going to do it. Just shut up and keep watch.

OK, round the back of the building, down the row of garages. We want the one at the end. Should be unlocked, unless he's got himself organized and fixed the door, which isn't likely. He's one disorganized gobbo.

Keep low. We can't relax just cos it's raining and

there's no one out. There's windows looking down on these garages. See 'em? Nebs live in there, nebs with eyes and yakky mouths.

I'm just hoping no one's looking out right now. Can't see anyone but we won't hang about. Right, here's the end garage. Check the door. What did I tell you?

Unlocked.

Know why? Cos two years ago I squirted a bit of superglue in the fitting. Not so you'd notice it—or he wouldn't anyway—but enough to bodge the mechanism. Door closes OK but it won't lock. He still hasn't got round to fixing it.

Not that I come here much. I only use the garage if my usual snugs are taken and I'm desperate for a doss. I break in here and sleep in the car. It's warmer and comfier than slapping it on the street with the other duffs. Easier too.

Cos he never locks his car either.

Pull up the garage door, nip inside, pull it down again. Good to be out of the rain, good to be hidden again. Don't touch the light switch, Bigeyes. We mustn't be seen. And anyway, I like the darkness. I need it right now. And I can see good enough.

Check out the car.

Eyesore, isn't it? Not quite a banger but give it a few months. Main thing is, it'll do the job. It's old, it's got no alarm, and it still looks just about legal so hopefully the porkers'll leave us alone.

The gobbo who owns it hardly uses it. How do I know? Cos I check the milo every time I come. And you know what?

It's only moved ten in the last twelve months. That's right—ten miles. I've been keeping the score. The petrol gauge has been three-quarters full for yonks.

Two years ago he used to drive it a bit more. Not far—just little trips—but enough to stack up the milo. This last year's been different. He's hardly touched the thing. Took me a while to find out why.

He's got a gammy leg.

He's an old gobbo, lives alone on the ground floor, doesn't get out much cos he can't. Shouldn't really have a car. There's no way he's safe on the road. He probably knows that but he's keeping it anyway, like lots of old gobbos hang on to stuff.

And that suits me.

Cos if he can't use the car, I can.

Haven't driven it before. I've just used it for the comfy seats and extra warmth when I've had to slap it for the night. But now it's time to let her loose. OK, open the door. Shouldn't be a problem. Like I say, he never locks it.

Shit, I don't believe it. Won't open. Try the other door.

Locked too.

What's going on? He must have come out here for something—not to drive, that's for sure—and then locked the door after him.

Never mind, we can sort it. He's got everything we need in this little den. If we can just find it in the dark. Check round the far corner. That's where he keeps his tools and stuff. Bit of a tip but it's all there.

Piece of wire, that's what we want.

This bit's too long. Check round. He had some cutters here last time. There they are. Right, trim the wire, bend it into shape.

Perfect.

Driver's door, pull back the rubber round the

window, squeeze the wire down the gap. Come on, you dimp, go in. Got it. Poke it down, feel for the catch.

This is stupid, Bigeyes. I'm losing my touch. I should be in the car by now. But I suppose I haven't done much of this for a while. When I was playing dead and keeping low, I just wanted to stay under the radar.

So I'm out of practice.

Click!

Gotcha. Open the door. Now, back to the tools. We want a screwdriver. Got to be the right type. This'll do. Jump in the car. Stinky bloody thing, isn't it? What's this under the driver's seat?

A woolly hat.

That wasn't here last time. And the torch has gone. He used to keep it under the dashboard. Maybe that's what he came out to the car for. He leant down, grabbed the torch, dropped his hat at the same time, then locked the doors and went.

Whatever.

I can use the hat anyway. Yeah, I know. Dronky but I need to keep changing the way I look. And that gives me another idea.

He used to keep an old overcoat in the garage.

There it is, hanging on a nail by the door.

Jump out, put it on. Bit cobwebby but it's warm and most of all it's old-fashioned. Got a hood too. Even better. Can't do any harm. OK, Bigeyes, this is it. We got to start her up. But we'll keep the door closed till the last minute. Right, screwdriver . . .

Dig it under the plastic surround on the steering column. Easy peasy. It's loose anyway. I love these old motors. Pull it off. Now, screwdriver again. We got to prise off the ignition switch.

Doesn't want to come. Shift, you bastard! Come off!

There it goes—one sweet little ignition switch.

Now for the hard work. We got to yank the wheel till we break the steering lock. I like this bit normally. Makes me feel good. Don't know why.

But I'm different about this one.

Maybe it's the gobbo. I've never spoken to him. He doesn't even know I exist. But it's like most of the nebs I watch. I feel like I know 'em. Some of 'em I don't care about. I just use their snugs, eat their food, read their books.

But this old guy—seems kind of nice. Bit spittled in the head but no mess to anybody. I feel a bit bad nicking his motor. Still, he doesn't need it any more.

And I do. Can't be sentimental about it.

Yank, yank, yank. This is going to be a scrap, Bigeyes. It doesn't want to go. Yank, yank, yank. It's not going to go, it's not going to go.

CRACK!

You beauty!

Out of the car, push open the garage door. Rain's heavier than it was. Suits me fine. Check round the site. Nobody outside, nobody watching, as far as I can see. But even if they are, we're going.

Back to the car, jump in, force the screwdriver into the ignition switch. Perfect fit. Like they were made for each other. Hold your breath, Bigeyes. This is the moment. It should work. It usually works. Choke out, twist the screwdriver and . . .

The engine roars into life.

Rev up, give her a minute, ease back the choke. Reverse gear—think it's push down and right. Got it. Handbrake off, clutch up. She's a juddery girl, this one, a skitty old dingo. But she's moving, slow, out of the garage.

Rain's spattered the back window already. Can't be bothered to look for the rear wiper. There's plenty of room behind me. But it's spuming down now.

We're outside. Check round. Nobody in sight.

Jump out, close the garage door, back in the car. Fiddle round for the wiper control. Found it. We're clear to go. And still nobody in sight.

Come on, Bigeyes. We got things to do.

Drives all right, this girl. Bit of a scraggy clutch but OK once you get to know it. Wish I could open her up, do some damage. I want to rag her till she screams. Might make me feel better.

But it's too risky. And this isn't a joyride. It's business. It's keep to the speed limit, drive steady, no mess. We don't want eyeballs on us. That's where the rain's helping. Hard to see out, hard to see in, and nobody much interested in us anyway.

Out of the estate and down Strickland Lane. I know what you're thinking. You're thinking why head for the bypass and not into the city? Well, tough. Think till your brain pops. You'll find out soon enough. I got other stuff to sort out.

If I can just get the radio working.

Haven't used it before. Never wanted to take the risk of being heard in the garage. Just hope it works. Clock says it's close on one so we should get something on one of the local channels.

'The news at one o'clock.'

Bingo.

'Police are still looking for a boy of about fourteen, known by the nickname Slicky, and a sixteen-year-old girl, named as Rebecca Jakes, in connection with the murder of teenager Trixi Kenton.'

They haven't found Bex. Shit, Bigeyes, she's still lying in a ditch.

'There have been fresh developments during the day. Following an incident in the early hours of the morning, police are now investigating a deserted van, though they are not confirming whether or not this has any connection with the missing pair. In a separate incident later this morning, a boy in a grey anorak was seen running from the back garden of a house in the

Hamforth area of the city. Police are very anxious to trace this boy, though they are not saying whether there is any link between him and the boy they are hunting in connection with the murder.'

No mention of Jaz at all.

I'll tell you what it means, Bigeyes. It means Paddy and the other gobbos are still free. Well, maybe it's what I wanted, sort of. Not the grunt and those other dregs. I could have done with them bobbed up.

But Paddy—I want him for myself. I want a second chance. And this time I'll get it right.

Left towards the bypass, right down Southlands Avenue. Radio's still on. They're talking about other stuff. I'm trying to think, trying to stay calm.

It's hard. Got me worked up again hearing all this. I keep wondering about Bex. I hate to think of her body getting wet.

And Jaz.

I keep thinking about her too.

Switch off the radio. Don't want to hear any more. Got to focus, got to stop spinning my head. Got to think what I'm doing or I'm bogged out. End of Southlands Avenue and here's another plug in my heart.

The junction with Britannia Road.

Right takes me out of the city. Five miles and I'm on the motorway and gone. Plenty of petrol. I could scrape it a long way before I dump the car. Only it's no good.

We've been through this, Bigeyes. We both know I'm not going.

Turn left. Do what you got to do. Off down the road, round the roundabout, and now it gets interesting. Cos this is where I'm going to blitz your mind, Bigeyes. You were starting to think you knew me a bit, right?

Don't shake your head. You were. Well, get ready to be amazed.

Down the road, past the school, past the shops, left at the end. See that lane? Leads off into the country. Runs for a couple of miles through fields and stuff and ends up at a little stream.

Remote spot.

And that's where we're going.

Yeah, I know. I got this fear of water. OK, this terror. I admit it. I don't mind having a shower or a bath in some snug cos I'm in control when I do that. I turn on the tap and I turn it off again. A river's a different thing if it's a big one like down by the docks. So's a lake. I keep away from stuff like that. And I don't even want to think about the sea.

But this stream's no bum gripe, first cos it's not that deep and second cos we're not going on the water or in it. Well, not really, not so it's a problem. Come on. I'll show you.

Down the lane, slow, steady. Nothing too jumpy. Not that there's much risk. Nobody comes this way much. That's why I chose it. And the rain's going to keep off any hard-crust fishermen.

I hope.

Got caught out once. Guy in long wellies, wouldn't shift. Had to wait for hours till he split. That's why I normally come here at night.

I need the place to myself. Too right I do.

Drive on, still slow. Dingo car's juddering again. Doesn't like the low gears. Like I say, I usually come here at night. And I don't drive. I nick a bike and ride out here. Only not all the way.

See that stile ahead? On the left, where the stone wall's a bit loose? Just past that there's a willow, then some bushes on the other side of the wall. You'll catch 'em in a moment.

There you go. Got 'em?

I heave the bike over the wall out of sight among the bushes, and walk the rest of the way. That's why we're stopping the car. Engine off, climb out. Rain's eased off. Nice timing.

Right, Bigeyes, we walk the rest of the way. No glumming. We walk.

No connection with the car. No connection with anything. Just a boy walking down a lane and hope-fully no one to see him.

Let's go.

Down the lane, slow as before, steady and slow. Dark, swirly sky, rain clouds but dry for the moment. Let's hope it stays like that a bit longer. We don't need much time. But a dry patch would be cute.

Last part of the lane. Twisting ahead, see? Another few yards and you'll hear the stream. Nice kind of sound, specially at night when there's a moon out, and maybe stars, and it's all quiet. I don't come here a lot but when I do, I like to hear the sound of the stream.

Makes the water feel less scary. Not much though. Follow the bend round to the right. Listen . . .

Got it? OK, bit further—now listen . . .

That's it. Soft, trickly sound. It's usually a bit louder. Maybe it's the breeze keeping it low. Come on, and keep your eyes moving. We should be alone but you got to watch. And remember what I said.

I'm going to blitz your mind.

You're going to be amazed.

There's the stream. Sweet little thing, isn't it, considering it's effing water. Walk to the end of the lane, turn right along the bank. Keep sniping round.

Looks all clear, like it usually is. I'd still rather have come here at night but we haven't got that luxury today. It's got to be now.

OK, nearly there. See that narrow bridge ahead? Tiny little thing half-hidden by gorse? It's only for walkers. It links that path coming from the right with the one on the other bank.

That's where the fisherman was standing that day.

And it's where we're heading now.

But slow like before, watching like before. We got

to be more careful than ever now. Cos there's lots to lose if we get this wrong.

Up to the little bridge, stop, check round. Now—climb down the bank, dip under. Bank falls away into the stream. Only what else do you see?

Three things.

First, the water's shallow—knee-height max. Second, the underside of the bridge is made of brick. Third, it's all nice and solid.

Only you'd be wrong.

Shoes off, socks off, roll up the trousers. Don't like this bit, Bigeyes. I know it's only shallow. I know I said it's not a bum gripe. But I still don't like it. What if I slipped over and hit my head on something? You can drown in a bath, remember. It's happened. I have to keep telling myself it's safe.

Brace up . . . into the water. Yi! It's got a chill like a frozen kiss.

'Come on, front up. Get used to it. Can't hurt me.'

That's it. Keep saying it. Can't hurt me, can't hurt me. It's too shallow. I just wish it would stop ripping against my legs.

Focus. Do what you got to do.

Right, Bigeyes, look ahead. Check out the under-side of the bridge. See the brickwork? Follow it down to about three feet above the water. Now check out the bricks again. What do you see?

Nothing. I can tell. You see beautiful bricks. An expert piece of building.

Now watch.

This one here . . . waggle it. Tiny bit loose. See? Bit more, now ease it out, slow, slow. Not too violent or we'll chew up the edge and make it clear the brick comes out. Got to be clever about this. Took me ages to make it look right.

There we go—out it comes. What do you see inside? A little empty space. That's cos I've taken out some of the other bricks. You've heard of a hole in the wall, right? Well, this is mine. And it's better than any bank.

Reach in, feel about, pull out the plastic bag.

Surprised? I knew you would be.

Check inside it. What do you find? Another plas-tic bag. And inside that . . . another one. And inside that . . .

Over ten grand.

There's work gone into getting that, Bigeyes. Lots of work over lots of time. And it's not from lifting wallets. I'm hot crack when it comes to that but there's other ways of making money.

And I got plenty. This isn't my only secret cupboard. There's more. I'm not telling you where. But I will tell you something. There's not just money in 'em.

Go on, reach in again, right to the bottom.

Another plastic bag.

Pull it out. Same again, bags inside bags. And what do you find at the end? Go on, tell me you're not blitzed.

Diamonds.

And they're not just any diamonds. Look at 'em. When did you see jewels like that? You probably never been this close to so much beauty. Or so much wealth.

Yeah, wealth. We're talking wealth, Bigeyes. The kind of wealth some people kill for. And remember what I said—this isn't my only cupboard.

OK, I've shown you. And now we put it back. That's right, we put it back. Can't take it with us. Too risky.

You can't carry this stuff round with you. It stays hid for another time. I came here for the ten grand.

Push the diamonds back in the cupboard, check the money again. Didn't want to have to break into this. I've been living good enough off what I lift. I was saving this for emergencies.

Well, this is an emergency. I got to do what I got to do, and then wig it out of the city. Got to hit some place I don't know that well and where I got to stay low. And I may have someone with me. I won't be able to nip out and cream wallets any time I feel like it.

I'm shivering in the water now. I want to climb out but I got to stay hidden under the bridge while I finish this off. Quick count of the money.

Ten thousand, four hundred, and sixty pounds.

How much to take, that's the question.

The lot. Take the lot. There's plenty more elsewhere. It's just that . . . I'm a bit cautious carrying so much, especially where I'm going. But then, maybe I just got to risk it. There might not be a chance to clock one of the other cupboards. I may have to blast out too quick.

And I'll need all the money I can find.

Take the lot.

Split up the money, push different bits into different pockets. My hand brushes the knife, closes round it. I feel another shiver. It's not like the shiver from the water. It's a different shiver. I let go the knife, pull my hand out.

'Come on. Get on with it.'

I stuff the empty bags back in the cupboard, wedge the brick in place again, check all's cute. Looks like it always did, nice and neat. And now—at last— out of this stinking water.

Up the bank, dripping, cold. Check round. Nobody in sight. All quiet. Just the breeze ruffling the grass and the trees along the top. Stop on the path, roll my trousers back down, pull on my socks and shoes.

Check again.

Still quiet.

Set off back down the lane. And now I'm getting nervous, Bigeyes. I don't want to choke out but I'm getting stressed. It's not just cos I don't like carrying all this money.

It's cos of the knife.

Just touching it again's brought everything back. It's not going to stop me going through with things.

Don't stick that idea in your pot. When it comes to it, you'll see what I am. I messed up before. It won't happen again.

Only this is it.

This is where it happens.

Reach the car, check all's clear, jump in, start up. No room to turn here or close to the stream. Hit reverse, ease the clutch. Bit of a judder but the old dame starts to move. I'm getting a cricky neck peering back but there's nothing else for it till we find a place to turn.

This gate'll do.

Back off the lane, change gear, forward, round, off. We're heading for the city.

And my thoughts are flying.

I should be thinking of my plan, thinking of what's going on around me, but I'm not. I'm thinking of the past. Those diamonds set me off. Never mind where they came from. It's none of your business.

But they set me off.

Set me thinking of Becky. Not the Becky lying in a ditch but the other Becky. My old sweet Becky. She shouldn't have died. She should be alive. Why does everybody I care for have to die?

She'd have been my age if she'd lived.

Think of that. Fourteen. Still a kid really, like me. Only she never made it past eleven. And the other Becky didn't do much better. Sixteen, like Trixi was. Still a kid too, sort of. And then Mary.

No kid, that's for sure.

But just as dead.

They all die, Bigeyes. One by one they slip away. What's going to happen to me? Am I going to slip away too? Maybe I'll be dead as well by the end of the day, money gone, dreams gone.

But I never had much in the way of dreams anyway.

I should have. Everybody should have dreams. That's why I like stories. They're all about dreams. Dreams of being someone else, somewhere else. In stories you can be anything you want. Just for a while, a few minutes or hours. You can escape.

But not now.

This isn't a story. And it's certainly not a dream.

It's starting to rain again. I'm glad. It'll help. Cos I got to stop blabbing now, got to start watching. We're in the outskirts but I want to keep to the quiet streets.

I know how to get where I want to go.

But we won't be alone. Remember that. There's other people'll be there too.

Paddy's not stupid. He'll know it's one of two things. Either I blasted out the city or I stayed. And if I stayed, then there's only one thing I'd stay for. And he'll know what that is.

What he won't know is that my hair's different, my clothes are different, I'm in a car. And that I'm still hunting him.

He won't know that.

Till it's too late.

More rain. I like it. I trust it. It's like the darkness. You can trust the darkness. You can stay hid.

Drive on, sniping left and right. Traffic building up as we head in. Check the clock. Quarter past three. Were we that long sorting the money?

Doesn't matter. It's now that matters and now's dangerous enough. What's worrying me is the porkers. Seen three police cars in the last two minutes. No fuss with any of 'em but I got to be careful, got to drive right.

Another two police cars. Jesus, Bigeyes, they're out

in force. I suppose I should have guessed. Trixi dead, gobbos on the loose, me on the loose. Maybe they've found Bex's body, maybe even Mary's. No wonder they're buzzing around.

Drive on, street after street. Two porkers standing outside the Royal Oak. They turn and watch as I pass. Check the mirror—they're staring after me. I got a bad feeling, Bigeyes. I got a really bad feeling.

Left into Sampson Street, down to the end, right at the crossroads. On, on. We're going too fast. I don't mean the speed. That's legal, that's perfect. I mean the time. It's moving too quick.

Cos I don't want to arrive. Not yet. I don't want to be there. But the minutes are falling faster than the rain. On, on, street after street. I can feel my anger building up again. It's mixing with the fear and I don't like it. I know this mix too well. It's like a cocktail.

Only you wouldn't want to drink it.

Anger and fear, anger and fear. I've felt those two all my life. I can handle one at a time. Put 'em together and I'm trouble.

I'm dangerous.

Already I'm feeling for the knife. It's in my pocket

pressed against some of the banknotes. I pull it out, one hand on the steering wheel.

'Put it back. Not now.'

But talking makes no difference. I don't put it back. I flick it open. I'm steering with my left hand, feeling the blade with my right. And I'm murmuring to myself.

'Paddy, Paddy, Paddy . . . '

I close the blade, slip the knife back in my pocket. Cos now I've seen something else—the entrance to Elmleigh Close.

Where the old dunny lives. Remember her, Big-eyes? Tammy's gran. If they're keeping Jaz anywhere, it'll be here. Only we got to be spiky now. Got to miss nothing. Cos we're not just watching the house. We're watching for the nebs who are watching for us.

Trust me, they're here. Can't see 'em but they're here. Don't ask me how I know.

Drive down, slow, normal, park at the end behind the skip. Check over the road. Recognize the house? We saw it from the lane last time. Looks pretty quiet at the moment.

Problem is, I'm starting to get this feeling.

I know they brought her here. Everything tells me they brought her here. Just as everything tells me there's eyes watching for me. I don't feel threatened yet and the car's ready to roar off the moment I sniff shit. But like I say, I'm getting this feeling.

That Jaz isn't here.

The door opens—and it's that gobbo from last night.

Riff.

It's no mistake. I only saw him in the dark but I caught him good enough. Got a better view now though.

One dimpy slug. About twenty, face like a thud. Heavy build but clumsy, lazy. You can see it all over him. He's no trouble, a total muffin. But he's not alone.

There's another gobbo coming out with him. I can guess who he is from his face—Trixi's brother. What did Bex call him?

Dig.

That's it. Twenty years old, she said, same as Slugchops. You don't want to cross him, she said. But I don't need telling. I can see that from his face too.

It's got Trixi's grime all over it. Different kind of dreg to Riff. Can't believe I've never seen him before. But there you go. Even with all my watching, I miss stuff.

They're moving down the road, slow, easy. Don't look choked about anything. Certainly not sniping round for trouble. But I am. I'm watching for them and I'm watching for the others.

Still can't see anything. But they're here, Bigeyes. I told you, they're here. I can feel 'em squeezing my heart. Look back at the two gobbos.

They've stopped by a car. No checking round. They just get in like everything's no sweat. Riff's in the driver's seat. Starts up the engine.

I turn the screwdriver in the ignition switch—then stop.

Too soon to start up. Too dangerous. The other eyes watching'll make the connection with Riff's car starting and mine straight after. They'll fix on me right up.

Give it a couple more seconds. Can't give it longer or I'll lose 'em. They're heading down towards the main road. I'm itching to start up. I want to keep 'em in view. Check round. Still no sign of any eyes.

But they're there, Bigeyes. I'm telling you, they're there. There's stuff even I can't see. Only now we got to go. Can't leave it any longer or Riff'll be gone.

Twist the screwdriver. Engine fires. Check round again. Nothing moving in the close apart from a kid riding his trike on the pavement.

Go.

First gear, handbrake, clutch up, ease off down the road. Riff's turned right and gone but I should see him when I hit the main road. On down the close, and then I hear it.

The sound of another engine behind me.

Check the mirror. No sign of anyone pulling out. There's parked cars both sides of the street. Can't see which one it is. Drive on, got to drive on.

Reach the main road. Still nothing to see in the mirror. Riff's moving down towards the city centre but he's caught in the slow lane. Check the mirror again.

Still nothing.

But I heard the engine. I definitely heard it. I can still hear it—I think.

Look ahead, search for an opening in the traffic.

Here's one. Into the gap, turn right after Riff. He's moving faster now, five cars between us, but I got him fixed. Check back.

Still nothing there.

But they're coming, Bigeyes. I just know it. They're coming for us. I reach into my pocket, squeeze the knife.

Sound of a horn to the right. I've drifted off my lane. Let go the knife, snap hold of the wheel, jerk left. A van slips out of my blind spot, red-haired gobbo at the wheel. Peers over at me, gives a finger, cruises past.

I'm shivering again, Bigeyes, like I was in the stream.

I got to focus, got to stay calm, got to drive good.

'Put the knife away.'

That's right. Talk aloud.

'Put it away. You don't need it yet. Time later. Right now you got to drive. And you got to watch.'

Traffic's speeding up again. I can still see Riff ahead. He's moving to the right lane, like he wants to turn off at the next lights.

Check mirror, move to the same lane.

Just two cars between us now and still nothing behind. Nothing that looks dangerous anyway. Just cars, cars, cars. But they're all dangerous, Bigeyes. Any one of 'em could be carrying the gobbos who want me.

And the gobbo I want in return.

But it's not just Paddy. There's something more precious I want too.

Sirens!

Shit, Bigeyes, don't tell me . . .

They're some way back. Can't see any lights in the mirror but there's cars pulling to the side to make room. Riff's turning right at the lights. They're on green. He's heading down towards the docks. Sirens getting louder. I can see a flashing light now, still a good way back.

It's porkers. I knew it. And I'm guessing they're for me. I'm sure someone's seen me. But I'm not hanging round to find out. I got to follow Riff anyway. Why aren't the cars in front moving?

Christ! The guy behind Riff's stalled. Riff's gone on and the rest of us are stuck here. And the lights are going to change any moment.

More sirens. There's two cars at least. I can see one

and hear the other. They're stuck too now, can't move cos of a truck taking up too much room, but they'll be clear the moment it shifts.

Cars in front of me are moving again, turning right one by one. Revs, clutch up, slip forward, but now the lights are turning red. Stuff it, I'm going. Can't lose Riff, whatever the risk.

Blare of horns from the oncoming cars. I'm halfway across the other lane and there's guys leaning out of car windows screaming at me. And then I'm round and racing for the docks.

Only Riff's disappeared.

Got to think, Bigeyes. There's all these turnings he could have taken. I'm just praying he's carried straight on. We'll have to chance it. The road twists a bit so he might still be hidden just ahead.

Foot down, speed up. Never mind the limit now. Got to take a risk. The old motor's groaning. Doesn't like this rattling about. At least with me jumping the lights there's a chance of throwing off the nebs who were following.

But somehow I don't think I'm that lucky. And they'll all have seen which way I went. They'll know

I'm somewhere near the docks.

There's Riff. Dead ahead, see? Taking his time like the world's going to wait for him. Or is he waiting for me?

I only just thought of that.

Is he waiting for me?

He doesn't look a smart gobbo. Nor does his mate. Hard but not smart. I don't think they've sniffed me. But there's the sirens again. And they're coming this way.

Riff's turning left down Riverside Lane.

I'm going straight on. Got to shoot clever here. Mustn't give 'em any idea they're being followed. I can take the next road and end up at the same place as Riverside Lane. Cos all these roads end up at the same place.

The docks.

Yeah, I know. Water again, effing bloody water. And this is deep stuff, big river stuff, not some spitty little stream. There's cargo ships put in here, load, unload and then haul off back to the sea. I try and keep away from this place.

But there's nothing I can do about that now.

Check the mirror. No porkers in view but lots of other cars coming after me. I want to look back, flick over the faces in 'em, but there's no time. I got to turn.

Left, down Maple Street, and there's the water at the bottom like an inky gob. I feel like I'm driving down a tunnel straight into it. I can see the sides of the street, the warehouses on either side rising over me.

And here's the wharf opening up. Warehouses drop back. Stop the car, check about me. Riff's motor's over to the left, parked outside the Dockside Diner. Dronky-looking hole if ever there was one.

They're going in.

Let 'em get out of sight, edge the car round to the right, park by the chandler's, get out. Rain's still coming down. Funny—I almost stopped noticing it while I was driving here. Hood up, get ready to go—and there's that feeling again.

Eyes watching.

Why can't I see 'em, Bigeyes? I don't miss stuff. I'm quick, I'm smart. Only I'm missing this. What's happening?

Face down, over to the diner, check through the window. Crowded with nebs. Men mostly, but a few women too—and a kid. Little girl, sweet face, sitting with an old guy at the far end.

But it's not the girl I'm looking for.

Riff's at the corner table rolling a cig. Dig's ordering something from the gobbo behind the counter. And now I've seen something else.

It's not what I came here for. But maybe it's what I need.

Tammy and Sash heading for the diner.

Got to move, got to be in place ahead of 'em.

Into the diner. I'm glad about the crowd. It swallows me up. Can't keep my hood up though. Looks suspicious. The change of clothes, the hat, the cropped hair with its new colour—that'll help a bit. But I got to use all my skill as well.

This isn't like lifting wallets in Café Blue Sox. There's nebs here who want to stiff me. But I'm OK so far. I'm hemmed round by hefty gobbos. Check about me, slow, cute.

Tammy and Sash are in the doorway. They won't go for the counter. They'll head straight over to Riff's table. Don't ask me how I know. Dig's there too now with a tray of pasties and chocolate.

Check the nearest table. Nobody sitting there but there's stuff from the last people waiting to be cleared away—two empty coffee mugs and a half-eaten roll. Grab the roll and one of the mugs. Check again.

The two trolls are still in the doorway. Tammy's bent over a cig trying to get her lighter to flash. Sash is standing with her, looking round.

Glances my way, then back at Tammy.

Did she see me, Bigeyes? Don't think so. She'd have come straight over if she had, or looked hard at me, or said something. She's not subtle enough to act like she hasn't noticed anything. She's not looking back, not speaking or anything.

Tammy's still trying to light her cig. Gobbo behind the counter tells her no smoking. She glares at him, puts the cig and lighter away, glares at him again. I'm pretty sure I'm OK.

I got to take the risk anyway, got to do it now.

Shuffle over towards the corner table. Got to be as spiky as I've ever been. They can't hurt me in here but I'm still stuffed if they recognize me. And it'll ruin everything I've come to do.

Table next to 'em's taken, two gobbos and a woman. Just as well. Can't sit too close. Next table's got a bearded gobbo at it. Old guy, wrinkled and smelly, reading the paper. I sit down opposite him, back to Riff and Dig. Grizzlebeard glances up at me, sniffs, looks back at his paper.

I put the roll and mug to my mouth, make like I'm eating and drinking. Behind me I hear the gobbos and the woman talking at the next table. Then, on the other side of 'em, Tammy's voice.

'Give us some money for a coffee.'

Dig answers. I just know it's him. Something about the voice. Too dangerous for Riff.

'You ain't supposed to be here.'

'It's cold on that hulk.'

Hulk. Hear that, Bigeyes? She said hulk. Dig again.

'I don't care.'

I hate this voice. There's something about it chills me. Low, slow, like it doesn't need to shout or hurry cos it knows it's going to be obeyed.

'I told you to stay. Both of you.'

'Xen and Kat are looking after 'er.'

'Needs all four of you.'

'No, it don't. She ain't no problem.'

'Needs all four of you.'

I'm thinking fast, Bigeyes. There's only so many ships and boats along the quay. Two or three of 'em could be called hulks. But there's more boats further down the river, and some of 'em are real wrecks. Not like they're sunk but they're not safe. They've been shoved out of the way to rot and nobody's got round to sorting 'em.

But they're snugs for some of the dross round this city—if you're into sleeping in a sieve. Question is—do I wig it now and go looking or hang about in case I hear a bit more? Sash pipes up.

'We'll go back.'

'Good girl,' says Dig.

'Good girl,' says Riff.

Yeah, yeah. Hear that, Bigeyes? What did I tell you? He's weak as piss, that Riff. Good girl, good girl. All he can manage is an echo of his mate.

'Nobody asked your opinion,' Sash snaps at him.

Think she agrees with me.

'Shut it,' says Dig.

She shuts it. But Tammy keeps on.

'Give us some money for a coffee and we'll go.'

'I give you some already this morning. What happened to that?'

'Ain't got none left. We had to buy milk and stuff. Come on, Digs.'

'All right, all right.' Sound of coins dropping on the table. 'But it's drink up quick and back to the *Sally Rose.*'

I stiffen.

Sally Rose.

Now she really is a hulk. But I got what I need. All I want now is for Tammy and Sash to take as long as they want over their coffee.

I keep my head down over the roll and mug. Grizzlebeard's glancing at me again. I give him a wink and he looks quickly down. Out of the corner of my eye I see Sash heading for the counter. Scrape of a chair behind me.

I'm guessing Tammy's sat down but I don't want to look.

I put down the roll and mug, stand slowly up, back to the table. I'm facing Sash now. She's standing in the queue by the counter and if she looks this way, I could be in trouble. She didn't recognize me last time but that means nothing.

Head down, slip past her, out the door.

Hood up against the rain and I'm hurrying round the front of the diner. Glance up at the window. No one watching from the corner table. Dig and Riff are leaning together, talking. Tammy's turned to shout something at Sash.

I'm gone.

Sally Rose.

One battered old tramp. Don't know what kind of cargo she carried in her working days. All she carries now is whatever duffs happen to be dossing there. I've never been much interested in who they were before.

But things are different now.

Past the derricks, past the busy end of the wharf, past the newer warehouses towards the old, deserted ones. Nothing much lives here, Bigeyes. All that moves is the river and we both know what I think of that.

Look about you. As dronky a dump as you'll find. It's a disease, this place. Water on the left, wasteland on the right—no trees, bushes, hedges, just scrawny grass and the carcasses of warehouses.

Can't see anyone following but that could change any moment. I got to keep checking. Can't stop for a second. There's enemies everywhere, even if I can't see 'em.

I'm checking the boats too. The decent ones are moored out in the river, the slaggy ones up against the bank. Couple of good 'uns close in but the rest are trash, barges and lighters mostly, rotting on their lines.

And here's *Sally Rose*.

Stop, check behind. Still no sign of trouble. Nobody on the path, nobody on the water, nobody round the derelict warehouses. Reach into my pocket, feel for the knife.

Xen and Kat.

I can handle them. As long as it's just them.

I squeeze the knife and there's that shudder again. Never used to be like that, Bigeyes. Used to be simple. Blade out and do it.

But I can't stop now. I got to go through with it. I'll be all right once I've started. The old habits'll kick in. I just got to make myself do it.

Walk on, fast, quiet, watching cute.

No movement anywhere, just the river licking past. I'm trying not to look at it. Plank from the stern reaching over to the path. Dodgy-looking thing and I'm not mad about walking down it with water underneath. But there's no time to hunt for something better.

It's got to be now.

Check round. Still no sign of anyone. Onto the plank, step forward. Bounces but it's OK. Don't look at the water, just eyes on the plank and keep walking, step, step, step.

I'm on deck.

Look around me. Nobody. Got to move soft now, dead soft. Listen hard. No voices, footsteps, no sounds at all. Hatchway on the other side, already open. Creep over, peer through.

All dark but a ladder stretching down into the boat.

Climb over, slow, quiet, ease myself down rung by rung to the bottom. I'm in the hold, darkness all round, but I'm starting to see clearer, I'm starting to hear voices.

Just a murmur but enough. It's the other two trolls.

They're in a cabin somewhere in the bows. Can't hear what they're saying but I recognize the voices.

Creep forward. I don't want the trolls. I just want Jaz. But if I got to fight, I will. And you know what's scaring me now, Bigeyes?

Me.

That's right. I'm scaring myself. Cos I can feel that anger coming back. I can feel myself breathing blood again. And you know why? Cos I'm suddenly seeing it clear. It's not just Paddy that's wrong.

It's everything that's wrong.

That's what's getting to me. Everything's wrong.

Rubbing out Bex was wrong. Nicking Jaz was wrong. All that's happened to me since the day I was born—all that was wrong. All that's still wrong.

And there's part of me wants Xen and Kat to come out. I'm squeezing the knife and I want 'em to come out. I want 'em to find me.

Cos they're wrong too. You listening to this, Bigeyes? They're wrong too. And if I can't have Paddy and all the others, I'll have them.

I'm up in the bows now and there's closed doors in front of me. The one on the right's got a taper of light round the edge. I can hear the trolls talking inside. But straight ahead's another door.

No light round the edge—just a bolt on the outside.

Drawn across.

The voices are still murmuring in the other cabin. Then suddenly they stop. But I don't care. It's too late now. And like I told you, I almost want 'em to find me. I draw back the bolt, open the door, gasp.

She's lying in the darkness, tied, gagged, eyes peering out at me from her battered face. But it's not Jaz.

'Bex,' I murmur.

Everything happens fast now.

The other door flies open. Xen and Kat jump out, knives drawn. Thump of footsteps on the deck above, wail of sirens far down the quay. I turn to face the trolls. They're keeping back, waiting for the others probably.

'We know who you are,' says Kat. 'Whatever you done to your hair and clothes.'

I don't answer. I'm watching 'em close but I can hear Bex behind me. She's crawled as far as the door. I reach back with the knife, cut the ropes round her wrists.

'Untie the rest,' I tell her.

And I'm watching the trolls again.

I can't take my eyes off 'em for a second. More footsteps above. They haven't come down yet. Maybe they don't know I'm here. Xen screams up.

'He's down 'ere!'

Voices above, sound of running.

I feel Bex pluck at my arm. I glance back. She's untied and ungagged herself and she's crouched there behind me. Her face is a mess. Nothing broken as far as I can see but they trimmed her up proper.

'I thought you were dead,' I mutter.

'Guy who killed Trixi knocked me out.'

'I heard him say he killed you.'

'He probably thought he did. He hit me hard enough. But I come to. And 'e was gone and Riff was standing there with Jaz. Then Dig turned up. You can guess the rest.'

So Paddy was boasting to his mates. All that stuff

about killing her and dumping the body. But she hasn't done much better since.

'Who did that to your face?'

'The girls.'

'Keep behind me,' I say.

Shadows in the hold now. Dig, Tammy, Sash, Riff. All got knives out except Riff. But they're not rushing me. They're spreading out.

'He's still got Trixi's knife,' says Xen. 'See?' She calls out to Dig. 'Be careful. He knows how to throw it.'

'So what?' says Dig.

And he flings his own knife, not at me but at a crate nearby. The blade thuds into the wood and the shaft quivers in the dark. He watches it for a moment, then pulls out another knife, a bigger one.

'Blade,' he murmurs in that slow voice. 'Guy told us your name. We was hoping you'd show up again.' He glances at his knife. 'So we can do right by Trixi.'

'I didn't kill her,' I say. 'The guy who spoke to you—'

'Told us everything,' says Dig. 'Nice polite gentle-man, most obliging. Though you wouldn't want to get on the wrong side of him, I'm guessing. Or his mates. He come and found us at Tammy's gran's. Said he'd seen Trix and the girls there once before when he was looking for you.'

'He's a liar.'

'Said he saw you kill her. And it's not the first time you killed neither. Said him and his mates have been looking for you for years and it's time for revenge. So we all went looking for you. Put the word round a few friends too. Kept in touch by mobile. Riff found you on the lane and rang us. Rest was easy. Or should have been. We done our bit. They cocked up theirs. But here you are anyway.'

'I didn't kill Trixi. Paddy did. The guy you spoke to. Bex was there. Ask her.'

'Yeah, like we're going to believe a word she says.' Dig scowls at her. 'She's never said nothing true all her life. That's why I'm finished with her.'

I glance at Bex again. She's staring at me with this haunted look. She nods suddenly.

'He's right. Him and me, we was . . .'

She falls silent. I look back at Dig.

'Yeah,' he says. 'We was. Only we ain't now.'

So that's how Bex got in the gang. It wasn't cos she was tough. I knew that anyway. It was cos she was Dig's girl.

My mind's starting to spin. I got to stop it, got to keep my head, got to remember what I came here for. I square up to Dig.

'Where's Jaz?'

He raises his eyebrow.

'Jaz?'

'Where is she?'

'You want Jaz, do you?' He glances at the others, chuckles. 'He wants Jaz.'

They chuckle too. He turns back, studies me with a leer.

'I don't think Jaz'll want you. Not looking like that. You seen your face lately?'

'Where is she?'

'She ain't going to want nothing to do with you.' He lowers his voice. 'Cos you look scary, boy. You're so angry you're spitting flames. You got a rage in your head like I never seen. It don't freak me out. But it's going to freak her.'

I'm trembling, Bigeyes. Cos I know he's right. I'm

breathing blood worse than ever. But I can still do it. I can calm myself for Jaz. And she'll trust me. She's that kind of kid. She trusts. She'll know it's me.

I got to get her away. Her and Bex. Dig's no father for her. She needs her mum. And she needs me. Whatever it takes, I got to get her away.

'Let me see her,' I say.

Dig gives me a smirk, then nods towards a door on the far side of the hold.

'Feel free,' he says. 'But don't say I didn't warn you.'

I look round at them all. They're watching me close, watching the knife in my hand. For all their numbers and Dig's bravado, they're scared of what I can do. I stare at the far door.

'Move back,' I say.

I see eyes flicker towards Dig. He nods. They move back, still watching me. I reach behind me, feel for Bex's hand. She takes it, holds it tight.

I lead her across the hold to the other side. No one moves, speaks. All's quiet, just the creak of the hull and the drumming of the rain on the deck above.

I reach the door, let go Bex's hand, check round at

the others. They're still standing there watching. I look back at the door. No taper of light but no bolt across either. If she's in here, she's no prisoner. Unless she's tied up.

I open the door.

And there she is. She's sitting on a little box facing out. She's got a pencil in one hand and a drawing book in the other, clasped to her chest. She's staring out with wide eyes. They fix on me, recognize me. I smile, murmur.

'Jaz, it's me, baby.'

She opens her mouth and screams.

It stuns me. I never heard a sound like it, never from her, never from anyone. Cos I never heard fear like it before. And I can't bear it. Cos I know it's what Dig said. It's fear of my anger, fear of my face, fear of me.

'Jaz, it's OK. It's me. It's—'

She screams again, louder.

'Jaz, I'm not going to hurt you.'

More screams. She's turning her face, twisting her body, like she wants to block me out. I lean in, touch her arm.

She jerks it away like I've scalded her.

'Jaz, listen.' I'm murmuring, whispering, desperate to reach her, desperate to break through her terror. 'Jaz, I've come to look after you. I got money and a car to get us away. You and me and Bex. We're going to be all right.'

I'm talking wild, promising the earth. It was the plan—the money, the car, the escape. It's not going to happen now with Dig and the others here but I keep talking anyway, keep trying to make her smile at me.

'Jaz, Jaz . . . '

She just screams again and again, then scrambles to the farthest side of the cabin, presses herself against the hull, hands over her ears, face dipped so she can't see me. I feel Bex pull me back, thrust the door shut. From inside the cabin the screams go on.

The others are moving close again.

'So this is where it all ends,' says Dig. 'And luckily I don't have to get my hands dirty. There's others to do that for us.'

He glances round at Riff, who's talking quietly on a mobile.

I'm still reeling. My mind won't work. All I can

think of is Jaz's screams, her face, her total terror—of me. I can't take that, Bigeyes. Not terror of me. Not Jaz. And suddenly it's like nothing else matters any more.

Only that's not right. There's still Bex. She still matters, even if I don't.

'Let Bex go,' I say. 'Do what you want with me. Only let Bex go. And let her take her kid.'

'I would,' says Dig. He pauses. 'If she had a kid.'

Silence. A deep, scary silence. Rain's stopped. So have the screams. I make myself speak.

'You telling me . . . ?'

'Ask Bex.'

I look round at her and there's that haunted face again.

'Tell me the truth,' I say.

'I love that kid,' she mutters.

'Tell me the truth.'

'We was good mates. We still is. We bonded cos I looked after her at Tammy's gran's. We're like dead close. There's nobody in the world she trusts more than me. And she's got no father. Ask Dig. The guy legged it. One-night stand and gone.'

'You haven't told me what I need to know.'

Another silence. I bellow at her in the dark, echoing shell.

'Who's Jaz's mother?'

She looks down, whispers.

'Trixi.'

I see Dig step forward. He's got trolls either side of him. They're like shadows now, all of 'em. I can't even see their eyes. But maybe I'm not looking. Cos somehow I don't care any more. No point in caring, no point in anything.

Jaz doesn't want me. And Bex is a dreg.

The shadows stop. Dig leans closer.

I see the big knife start to move. It hews the darkness as it gathers pace. I see my thoughts scatter before it, pricking my mind with tiny screams. Duck, they tell me. Dodge, parry, do something. There's time.

I know there is. I've been here before. But I don't move. I just watch, my own knife dead in my hand.

I feel a hot pain as the blade scores my brow. Blood fills my eyes and I fall to the floor. I hear screams, Becky first, then Jaz behind the door. Then I'm screaming too.

I hear the trolls start to yell, feel 'em crowd round. Then the kicks come thudding in. I curl up into a ball. A hand grabs my hair, yanks my head up.

I'm staring through the blood into Dig's face. I'm still holding Trixi's knife. I want to stab it right through him but I can't move and he knows it.

He gives a grin, then suddenly I'm jerked up on my feet and he's bundling me through the darkness. The trolls are still packed round me, punching, kicking, scratching, but I don't notice 'em now, don't notice anything, just the ladder thrust against my eyes.

And I'm scrambling up, Dig's knife prodding me on, and then I'm out on deck and the rain's drizzling down again, and I'm staring about me, trying to think. But my mind's split open and I'm fumbling through a fog.

Dig's on deck now, and the trolls, and they're closing round me again, kicking and shoving me towards the plank. I blunder over it onto the bank and stagger down the path.

They don't follow. They're still on the *Sally Rose,*

jeering at me. And somehow I can hear Jaz's screams again. Maybe they're inside my head. I don't know. All I know is that she doesn't want me.

I turn and totter down the bank. Blood's flowing worse now and my head's thumping. I know I'm badly hurt. I see porkers down the path, checking out the wharf. But they're the least of my problems.

There's two gobbos climbing out of the nearest barge. I recognize 'em. Lenny and the grunt. They've obviously been keeping out of sight of the porkers while they wait for me to show up.

Check round.

Third gobbo coming up behind, fourth to his left covering the waste ground, fifth climbing out of a lighter further down.

No sign of Paddy.

But what does that matter now, Bigeyes? It's all over anyway. I'm never going to get Paddy before they get me. Cos I'm finished, you understand? I'm totally effing finished. I can still run a bit but where to? Where can I go? I got a hundred yards in me, maybe two.

Even if I wanted to give myself up to the porkers,

I couldn't reach 'em. They're too far away, they haven't seen me and I got no voice left to shout.

I got one choice left, just one. That crumbly old warehouse. Probably won't get there before they catch me and even if I do, there's nowhere much to hide. But what else can I do?

Run, run.

Only it isn't a run. It's a lurch. I'm hurting bad in the head now and the blood's rushing down my face. I still got the knife but it feels useless, as useless and spent as I am.

Look back.

They're coming after me, all five. Not hurrying. Why should they? They know I can't get far. Shuffle over the scraggy grass, through the entrance to the warehouse.

Like I told you, nowhere much to hide. But if I can just get across the storage room and out the far window before they see me, they might think I've gone into one of the old offices.

Trouble is, I'm struggling bad now and the blood's making it hard to see. But I'm halfway over the storage room and still no sign of the gobbos. Few more yards and . . .

The window.

Shattered long ago, thank God, and beyond it the waste ground on the other side of the building. Check round. Gobbos not here yet but they won't be far away.

Squeeze into the window, slow, heavy. I'm moving like a dead weight, grazing my legs on the spikes of glass still left in the frame. Then suddenly I'm through and outside again.

Only I can't move. I'm slumped against the wall, I'm pouring blood, and I can't get up.

I hear sounds on the other side of the wall, footsteps moving about the storage room. Hard to tell how many of 'em are in there. I don't give two bells anyway. Nothing I can do any more. I'm not going to make it even if they don't find me.

But they have found me.

There's a figure walking this way.

Easy one to recognize. My old friend the grunt. He's come round the outside of the building and he's strolling down towards me, nice and easy, nice and slow.

Yeah, that's right. No need to rush now, big guy.

Just as well cos you're not that fit, are you? You're all on your own and I can see right into your mind. Even with my head drummed, I can read your little brain.

You're thinking, I don't need to call the others. I'll sort the kid on my own.

He's close now and you know what, Bigeyes? I'm clutching the knife and I'm wondering. He's moved away from the wall to skirt those nettles and now he's walking towards me.

Straight on.

I couldn't miss him if I wanted to. He's the biggest, fattest target in the world. I still got the strength, just. One throw and he's down. Easy, easy.

Does he know how much danger he's in?

Obviously not cos he's coming straight on. I squeeze the hilt, finger the blade, whip my arm back ready. He stops. He's just a few yards away but if he moves, he's a dead man. And he knows it now.

I call out to him.

'Where's Paddy, fat man?'

I don't expect an answer. But he gives me one in that thick, grunty voice.

'Helping the police with their enquiries.'

Christ, Bigeyes. They got him after all. I never thought that would happen. Least my tip-off did something. But I still wish I'd killed him. The grunt sniffs.

'Ain't going to help you much though.'

He's right. There's figures appearing both sides now. The other gobbos. They walk slowly round and stare down at me. I'm still holding the knife ready.

'Go on, then, kid,' says Lenny. 'Throw it.'

I want to, Bigeyes. I want to throw it so bad. Only I can't. I'm streaming blood and I'm crying. Crying for Jaz, crying for me, crying for everything that's never going to be.

I see 'em step forward but it's all a blur now. I don't know what's happening any more. I feel the knife twisted out of my hand, feel 'em poke through my pockets, pull out the money, joke, laugh.

Then the blow. It shatters the light, drowns my head. As I slip into the dark, I see Lenny lean towards me. Suddenly there's a crack—a sharp, heavy sound I've heard before.

Only I'm not thinking, Bigeyes, I'm not right. Everything's jumbled, everything's mad. Another crack. And this time I recognize it.

Gunfire.

Have I been shot? I don't know, Bigeyes. Cos nothing makes sense now. I can't feel my body. I'm drifting like breath through a murky space. I don't know who I am, where I am, what I am. But I hear a voice—low, distant.

'Blade,' it says.

I know it right away.

Mary.

tim bowler

BREAKING FREE

In the next instalment of Blade . . .

*Ever wondered where you go when you're dead?
Then watch this space. Cos I've been there. And
here's something to blitz your mind.
    I'm still there.
And I might not be coming back.*

He's found me, he's got me. That's trophy number one. Trophy number two will be bringing me in. But he doesn't want that. Too much trouble. And not enough fun. He wants trophy number three.

Taking me out.

Open my eyes. Still dark. Night's fallen over me like a cold kiss. But I can see the sky clear and good. I'm lying on my back, and I'm shivering and crying, and my body's hurting, and I'm looking up at the sky. And there's stars out. And a moon. A big, bright, funnyface moon. God, it's beautiful.

'Blade,' she says, 'you've got to give yourself up. Are you listening? You've got to face up to the law. You've got to face up to yourself.'

Tim Bowler is one of the UK's most compelling and original writers for teenagers. He was born in Leigh-on-Sea in Essex and after studying Swedish at university, he worked in forestry, the timber trade, teaching and translating before becoming a full-time writer. He lives with his wife in a small village in Devon and his work-room is an old stone outhouse known to friends as 'Tim's Bolthole'.

Tim has written eight novels and won twelve awards, including the prestigious Carnegie Medal for *River Boy*. His most recent novel is the electrifying *Frozen Fire* and his provocative new *BLADE* series is already being hailed as a groundbreaking work of fiction. He has been described by the *Sunday Telegraph* as 'the master of the psychological thriller' and by the *Independent* as 'one of the truly individual voices in British teenage fiction'.